An Essential Book of Good

☺!!!!~

An Essential Book of Good

☺!!!!~

An Essential Book of Good

By, P'fessor Guus

Edited by, H.F. Nugent

~ This Book

This book is a Journey of Good Clean Fun. This story is about two amazing friends as well as others living, learning and enjoying themselves while also learning about the many great lessons that this world has to offer them. This book is truly "An Essential Book of Good". Please enjoy the fun, wisdom and time tested lessons that have been carefully crafted for your edu-tainment.

~ About the author

With a birthplace confirmed as being on planet Earth, P'fessor Guus is a globally, ecologically and ethically minded person who has travelled the world extensively with all levels of humanity. P'fessor Guus' life's purpose is to bring imaginative, experiential edutainment to those that wish to be free thinking minds of the world. As the creator, P'fessor Guus, our author aspires to assist readers to open new pathways to attainable heroes, attainable lifestyles, attainable goodness, attainable world betterment and attainable experiences, with joy in mind for all. The Y&M series of books is for readers of any age who wish to imagine, create and expand their horizons. You may have met or dreamt of, or will meet P'fessor Guus someday soon. He's an author for *all* to enjoy and fully believes that "everyone is truly

4

amazing", and he's also quite grateful to meet people who have found their own amazingness and are open to sharing that amazingness with the world. You are truly amazing, so be amazing for the good of one and all today!!!☺~

~ Dedication

To Faith and Liberty, and my amazing wife — love of my life and great family creator ... thank you.

This book is dedicated as a thank you to all the amazing people that continue to "dream hard enough to make their dreams come true". To all wave-riders, sun-dancers, bodysurfers, stand-up surfers, lie-down surfers, knee and drop-knee surfers, fashion surfers, sand dune surfers, street and snow surfers, dance floor surfers, peaceful surfers, music surfers, life surfers, hand surfers, internet surfers, air guitar surfers, stock market surfers, more blessed, young and new surfers, pet surfers, canvas surfers, dream surfers, caring surfers, dirt surfers, health and wellbeing surfers, happy surfers and those that wish to be happier surfers, wishing-to-be surfers, used-to-be surfers, and even those that don't want to be surfers ... because you are all truly amazing and love is for everyone. So have fun, enjoy life and help others to enjoy life too!

~ Contents

~ Introduction

~The golden envelope~

Always remember that "good love" is what we all need. If you only want to hear about good things then email Yucckie and Mahzie, and for you, I and me, good love is what they will always be.

~Introduction

So together we raise our water glasses and say "Cheers & Thank you" for all future and past perfect powder days, plenty of glassy-tube time, smooth, empty car park concrete under our wheels, many exciting new things to learn, safe travels and good friends.

"Once upon a time", in some great stories, may have been quite true. However, in this particular tall tale, which may have seemed to happen in a time and place much closer to you, could also be true. Why, even as near as just yesterday in a land not so far away, and quite possibly just at the end of your street or one quite similar, you might come to say. In this place there lived a young, confident, kind, intelligent, joy-filled boy named "Yucckie", who some have said was also quite cool. "Cool" was always such a funny word to Yucckie, as cool was not cool unless, one really cares for all things, beings and even non-beings and their feelings of comfort, inclusion and their joy. If one did not care about others then cool was just another word for someone who had been fooled and didn't really know where they were going or where they had been, and wasn't really a leader but simply someone who needed some good, close friends to know and to care for them.

Yucckie always remembered, and included everyone, and he never forgot to let him or her know how much he cared for him or her while they were with him, as opposed to when they were not. This, being loved and cared for, is an extremely important thing for everyone's healthy and happy heart.

No one really knew why his name was Yucckie, or what country or language the name came from. "Faith" a young neighbor of his, was once heard to say that the name "Yucckie" is quite funny because it has a "Yuck" in it, which to some sounds not so nice or even a bit smelly or messy, about Yucckie none of which was true. Faith loved Yucckie no matter what some have said was the meaning of his name.

Now Faith and her sister Liberty were faced with a homonym dilemma and they decided, after meeting Yucckie and getting to know the way that he was, that they needed a new word to take the place of the word "yucky" that to many people meant something not so nice. So they created a new word they thought would not offend — not me, not you, not once, not even twice. From then on until the end, the word that would take the place of yucky would be "Gooby-gew" (*that was, of course, until they met someone with the name Gooby-gew, but the chances of that were far between and few*). They also liked Yucckie, because although he was a little more mature in years, he would always make time for them and sit without a problem, with only joy, while watching their favorite TV programs, which he of course knew all the dance moves and songs — he may even have owned one or two of the promotional toys. Yucckie was known to have a special place in his heart for any cartoon character, kid or adult, which practiced the art of infinite peaceful optimism or as Yucckie calls it "Opti-Mystics". Opti-mystics are his favorite thing to practice each and every day. Yucckie has always believed that solutions to any and all perplexing situations are only found with an optimistic approach, which is why he uses optimism for all things equally, not one or just two situations, but for all infinitely.

Interestingly enough, being that Yucckie was and still is such a wonderful, light-hearted fellow, who brought and brings happiness and sunshine to all that he met or could meet, back then most would never bother to ask him what his name meant or where it had come from. If this name was told in full, most would have struggled when trying to pronounce it in totality, which may be why it was shortened to Yucckie. The long version of his name is a name not many have ever heard or will ever come to know is my bet (*at least not many have enquired or have asked ... not many as of yet!*). I heard that once he *was* asked, which caused him to think

10

on the answer for quite a long while. In Yucckie's mind the organic processes flashed with an electric liquidity and a profundity that was unique to him. He spoke of this thought and finally said that neither he nor his name were from a set location, language, or land but rather of the places and people that inspired him. If there *were* such a geographical place of origin, the only name for it that Yucckie could muster would be something like this:

Euromeraustralasiafricartiscandichinussatlantitalacificiginewzeali relascoticejapanicaindiamazonileuphratiarctica?

This very unique sort of name would quite possibly be the name of the landmass on the Earth when the continents reconnect and people fully realize the true reason and need for sharing the Earth wisely and quite kindly.

Yucckie also noted that, as his body was approximately 80% water, which allowed him to be strong, brilliant, weak and powerful all at the same time, that he was definitely born more of the water than of the land. This is why, before he consumed it, he thanked every glass of water for its amazing life-giving power. Yucckie and his best friend Mahzie (*who you will also get to know*) were grateful for life and all it had to offer.

11

So it happened, that both Yucckie and Mahzie became icons for goodness, happiness, peace, knowledge, love and sharing (*at least that's what I've heard from many, many people from different lands*). How, you may ask? Read on folks and you will come to know the ways that they were, as well as their calm perseverance and simple kindness cures.

Yucckie and his "best friend forever" (*BFF*) by the name of Mahzie, created fun and happiness wherever they went, or wherever they could imagine to be or to go. It was said that one or both could pick up just about anything. A piece of aluminium, some old mattress springs, and a tin can — you name it. If they found it they could turn whatever it was into some strange or "kaswizzeling",[1] fun sort of thingamabobicle that would make someone's otherwise boring day into a new and surprising adventure, or simply a day of some much-unspoken and much-needed fun. These two, when together, could create an adventure for themselves and always included a "you" or an "I" with a forever up-standing and togetherness philosophy to never leave anyone sad, left out or behind.

---

[1]{ for kaswizzeling & other new words please refer to the Philo- Glossary in the final pages of this book]

While Mahzie's electronically- and intuitionally-gifted story is quite incredible, Yucckie's description for your mind to comprehend is the focus of this particular book that you are reading to its end. The way of Mahzie is a story of mathematical logic that you will learn about in other ways. One interesting fact about Mahzie that *can* be revealed is that many around him don't know if he ever uses his eyes. In fact, nobody has ever seen what's behind his thick black bangs, or as some call it, his thick hair fringe. Surely he can't see out of this fringe if nobody else can see in?

To find a solution around this predicament, he did find a way. Mahzie created a thing that he called the "Uni-directional, I-Locational, A-Triangulational Sensor Necklace", or UDILATS to make it quite simple for those that like things to be short. The UDILATS was amazing! This UDILATS necklace when worn, created a super-sensitive force field around it's wearer, that could assist a person who cannot see with their eyes allowing them to walk anywhere, anytime with out having to worry about anything threatening their lives!

But now back to Yucckie. He was and is neither short nor tall, fine nor rough, wide nor thin, light nor dark, or even stylistically out or in. He is just somewhere in the middle which is quite suitable to all and of course, just right for him. The most

13

memorable things of this wonderful boy are his forever-present warm smile and his love-gifting eyes that never let anyone feel forgotten or left behind, and somehow gave or gives a special feeling that one will always in him, have a friend.

Yucckie was, is and always will be someone in whom almost anyone can honestly, happily and comfortably confide. The comforting look in his eyes is that of everyone's closest and most familiar friend, which makes everyone want to meet with him again and again and again. Yucckie's hair isn't straight, combed or curly — it's really all kinds of styles and colors but quite natural and fitting for him (*and, much like the rest of Yucckie, where he was from, you just could not pin*). Perhaps this is why Yucckie is so familiar to all, and almost everyone's friend and if he isn't yet, he will be soon when he comes back to meet you again. It's really quite funny that his name is Yucckie, because he's anything but.

I'm sure it can't be because of the food sometimes left on his shirt, with just a bit of a smirk, a smile or a big toothy grin (*about this food he would say, "it is being saved for a little snack for later in the day"*). But about his name, I heard through the grapevine, through a friend of a friend of a friend of a friend that because of this world that we live in, he simply had to shorten his name — it was so long before that anyone could understand this reason for a

14

change for sure. His name is said to be this one of odd sorts, which is difficult even for *him* to pronounce and was also so hard to make short:

Yucckioguchihaakonsmithslaterocurrenolupokahanmkunugentbuck nertonsenjacobsmithwilliamhayesperkinhawking (and so muchly much more!)

Now that this name has left your and my mouth and even our jaws on the floor, of this I am quite sure: this name and this word will mean something much different to you by the time this sweet and buttery story has been spread around this great blue and green Earth. This remarkable young boy is a bit cheeky, but still quite organized and clean. Yucckie enjoys quite muchly to surround himself with anything and anyone that is honest, happy, caring and wants a life of "good, clean fun", otherwise known as GCF. (*Fun can, of course, never be at the expense of another person or that person's feelings*). GCF is the kind of fun that can be shared by all, laughing, chuckling and giggling *with* one another and never *at* one another. Yucckie likes to spend time with folks who can share their knowledge and their stories of adventures, of searching or finding the most sought-after universal treasures. All of these treasures in Yucckie's mind must be from a foundation of simple and courageous acts of

15

unconditional love, kindness and again of "GCF".

Fortunately, Yucckie is endowed with a natural, magical propensity for unconditional love and kindness (*yes, that is what I said — the magical power of LOVE!*). Don't be afraid because, real love is truly amazing. Never make the mistake of thinking that love is a weakness. You'll find out soon enough that love has the ultimate and maximal power to correct all that's wrong and make it magically right. Love is a universal equalizer for everyone and all to live with in delight.

Yucckie could & can, always and quite uniquely find ways to re-lighten or brighten the light in a heart where that light may have almost gone out or become tired or dim. From even his earliest memories, Yucckie recalled that his parents kindly instilled this great thought process deep within him. As long as unconditional love was in his heart, his path would be clear and his actions would flow with a simple, natural, sparky spontaneity. This natural spontaneity was quite obvious in his style of riding the great oceans, mountains and concrete waves of the streets, that he could ever so effortlessly carve, always dawning his signature, content, warm and happy smile.

The simple act of giving the gift of a warm smile can be the perfect way for anyone's day to begin or to end. The effects of offering a smile from a travelling car, plane, bus or boat can last for more than a thousand minutes, hours, days, kilometers or miles. Yucckie says that not everyone knows that the word "smiles" is in reality the longest word in the English language. Why do you ask? Because it's the only word with a mile between the "s" at the beginning and the "s" at the end! Maybe that's why a simple smile can be so amazing and can surely create a great new friend for life.

So accompany you, I will today on this journey, for some interesting fun with all of Yucckie and Mahzie's friends and friends-to-be. This journey will continue on and on for as long as you stay in friendly contact with Yucckie and Mahzie. Don't worry if English is not your mother tongue — both Yucckie and Mahzie love language adventures, of that I am very sure as "Making New Friends in Any Language" is one of their favorite self-made songs. When you write to Yucckie and Mahzie they will translate your great words as well. This translation will then open a brand new Y&M adventure door and possibly another great story to live, to hear or to tell. With so many languages in the world available to them, you and me, language translations will make it possible for you to meet and to share stories both on and offline with the very open minds and hearts of Yucckie and Mahzie.

~Talking to the world

It's important to be aware of just how many languages are out there or even to know just the most well known twenty, thirty, forty or so. If you will, just look at this list below, as it will help you to understand just how many there are to learn or to try to know. You may need to sing them in a song. Just to remember a few, or even 20 or more, begin with this list we provided for you;

Mandarin, English, Spanish, Hindi, Russian, Arabic, Portuguese, Bengali, French, Malay, German and Japanese. Farsi, Urdu, Punjabi, Wu, Vietnamese, Javanese, Tamil, Korean, Turkish and Telugu are languages too. Marathi, Italian, Thai, Burmese, Cantonese, Kannada, Guajarati, Jin, Min Nan, Persian, Polish, Pashto, Xiang, Malayalam and Sudanese. Hausa, Oriya, Hakka, Ukrainian, Bhojpuri, Tagalog, Yoruba, Maithili, Uzbek, Sindhi, Amharic and Fula. Romanian, Oromo, Igbo, Azerbaijani, Awadhi, Gann, Cebuano, Dutch, Norwegian, Navajo, Finnish, Swedish, Kurdish, Inuit and Cherokee. Kurri, Malagasy, Croatian, Saraiki, Nepali, Sinhalese, Chittagonian, Zhuang, Khmer, Assamese, Madurese, Somali, Marwari, Magahi, Haryanvi, Hungarian, Chhattisgarhi, Greek, Chewa, Deccan, Akan, Kasakh and Min Bei. Sylheti, Zulu, Czech, Kinyarwanda, Dhundari, Haitian Creole, Min Dong, Ilokano, Maori, Quechua, Kirundi, Hmong, Shona, Uyghur,

18

*Hiligaynon, Mossi, Xhosa, Belarusian, Balochi and Konkani.
British, Australian, American, Canadian* — even in English there
are many different meanings and thoughts as well as ways of
speaking.

There are, of course, so many more to learn, each with
almost endless different slangs and dialects, with thoughts and
meanings that may change if one is to add one's own style or a
little bit of cheek. You may learn as many as you can, especially if
you're keen to travel to many lands, searching for as many friends
as Yucckie and Mahzie have, which is a friend collecting number
that may change from year to day to week. Important it is to learn
languages that are different from your own, and at a minimum to
say "hello" and "thank you" in three or four or so. If your language
was left off of our list don't fret or be sad, just send it in an email
and Yucckie or Mahzie will be sure to try to learn about it and will
truly be thankful to you and will also be very glad!

In this brave new world of maps, GPS and automated
compasses, the old ways of meeting new people or even the lucky
discoveries that sometimes come with getting lost are being
forgotten and sadly considered odd or bad. So if your language is
missing from the list, let this be another lost lucky moment for all
of us to be happy to have had. We can count ourselves lucky for

19

finding this lost, but now found, remarkable moment as the reason for all of us to have met.

In your future or even your travels of now, please remember not to be in too much of a hurry. Knowing that the earth is quite round, it may quite possibly be an ongoing great adventure. If you use this rule of thumb which may prove very profound: when going north, use the southern route and when travelling west try the eastern path, as no matter which way you go, if you go for long enough, you will end up going in the direction that you originally intended! Your end, if you walked quite straight on this beautiful squircular sphere, may even be right back at your start. Carry with you a mind and heart, wide open and surely you will gain great stories and a more universally loving, sharing, caring, compassionate & happy heart. From Yucckie and Mahzie's perspective, sharing this great world is inevitable. They believe it's best to have this "sharing" knowledge from life's very beginning, so that each of us can also have respect and care for all of the world's souls and hearts.

~Sharing is inevitable

Both Yucckie and Mahzie realize that the nature of the Earth's shape is most obviously a simple lesson in sharing, otherwise it wouldn't be so squircular. The shape alone causes us to have to share. The nature of a squircle is that it shares the beginning, the end and both the within and the without. Therefore we must all care about sharing happily, of this there is no doubt. We share the same air — there is no way around it. We also share the same water, whether we are quenching our thirst with it, showering in it, using it to pour concrete (*to skateboard on it*), making spaghetti out of it, washing our clothes in it, sliding on the slippity-slide through it, putting out a fire with it, singing in the rain in it, swimming through it, watering our garden with it, sailing or rowing a boat across it, wake-skating on it, SUP-ing across it, fishing in it, scuba diving under it, getting our golf balls out of it, making water balloons with it, snowboarding or surfing on it, or even getting splashed by Yucckie's (*not so friendly*) friends Arro and Gance in the pool with it. It's just a fact of life that we must share while living on a squircular planet, so why not share it all happily! It seems so easy (*unless, of course, you are Arro or Gance*).

Arro and Gance are OK when they're apart but when you put the two together things never seem to go well (*but that's another story that will take some time to tell*).

Just the other day, a sharing moment caused Yucckie to notice this share-o-logical concept in another way. Yucckie noticed something interesting while surfing the oceans waves. When he's sitting in the line-up waiting for a wave to come to him, sharing is a magically natural occurrence, one that we really cannot escape. We may as well just let it happen by going with the flow of the universal natural currents and enjoy it in the happiest of ways.

In his great surfing memorized moments that also created great awareness and enlightenment. Yucckie was glad to have his eyes and mind wide open, as a legendary surfer by the name of Midget Farley floated over an unbroken swell way "out the back" or further out to sea than the rest of the surfers in the ocean sat. Then another one of Yucckie's heroes by the name of Barton Lynch, along with the entirety of his complete "Grom Squad" floated over the same lifting swell. Mahzie was also lifted high by this same ocean swell but was too far out to catch it. Milli-seconds later, Mahzie called out to Yucckie and screamed out "Go, Go, Go Yucckie Go!"

Just then three dancing dolphins submarine-surfed this swell as if they were guiding it and delivering it over to Yucckie! This great, shared swell was now cresting and getting ready to break. As Yucckie paddled for it, it seemed that this ocean swell was a gift to enjoy from without and within. Yucckie paddled with strength and grace as he lifted the sky with his back and allowed gravity to drop his board down the wave's face as he caught, carved and rode this great shared gift of a wave all the way across a shared shallow sand bank, with those same dancing dolphins riding the curling under-wave, as if they were also his best surfing mates. This wave couldn't have been better if he had dreamt it!

With the tide changing all throughout this day, the sandbar on the bottom created even better wave conditions for Yucckie, Mahzie and the rest to happily share more and more perfect waves. That day, the incredible surf-carving and dolphin wave magic created stories for them all, as well as for those on the cliffs above and many unknown sunbathers who watched from far beyond. All of this great sharing was created with just that one single wave. That amazing swell moment that Midget, Barton, Yucckie, Mahzie and the dolphin's rode, was to be re-ridden and passed on as a gift-giving story for infinite minds and memories. A gift that could and would be shared by the brain waves of happy thoughts that could help the whole world to feel quite joyful for as long as these stories are taught or told.

Instantly, that same surfing wave was transformed into electrical brain waves, which (*like all brain waves*) can carry memories, and dreams that can be re-ridden in the limitless capacities of infinite imaginations. When any brain waves are translated into spoken stories, they will go far beyond the limits of our own minds or even anyone's special beach in time. Another great thing about brain waves is; nobody knows what a brain wave weighs, but I am very sure you can't currently measure one on a luggage or postal scale, hence one can travel with it free of charge — at least that's how it is today and most likely all of the inevitable tomorrows or until someone invents a way to weigh a brain wave.

Connected....You, I and we are in sharing. From the smallest to the tallest, the widest to the thinnest, the sleeping to the awake, we are connected. When we become aware of this great fact, then all of us together will have the greatest love-filled hearts every single day of our lives (*we simply need to share the end, the in-between and even the start*).

With so many different ways of speaking, being and living, we're lucky to live on a squircular or roundish planet that can keep us all connected (*even if we aren't aware, from our humble birth or start*) of the great joy of sharing. Yes we are, and always will be connected by the water we drink and the wonderful air created by the many plants and trees that we share and truly need for all life to be and to breathe. What an interesting fact for you and I to know and to believe, don't you think?

If, say, the Earth were another shape, with un-crossable gaps, gullies or canyons, we may never make those faraway friends at all (*at least until someone designs a gap-, gully- or canyon-crossing smart phone app*). Essentially, this is what the Internet is. To Yucckie and his friends, the internet creates a chance to meet and to share the world while just sitting on our bums, giving us all much stronger fingers and thumbs. It's quite lucky for the you's, I's and me, that this isn't the only way to travel but just one way, if and when travel and meeting people indeed becomes a need.

Our Earth is a Squircle or squircular in fact. Squircular, by Yucckie and Mahzie's definition, is:

> **Squircle or Squircular** — *a bumpy, odd-shaped circle or sphere endowed with the perfection of many imperfections; including but not limited to rounded; squares, rectangles, triangles, octagons, pentagons, pyramids, and not-so-pointy pointy things.*

A squircular shape for a planet is great: all one has to do is keep walking straight and one will eventually arrive where one began while hopefully making amazing friends on the way or even a great new Australian or non-Australian mate!

Yucckie and Mahzie discovered during a long road trip across Australia that Australia is known for some of the longest roads in the world! These roads are also endowed with the longest parts that are straight (*so if you don't like making turns, starting your journey there, may for you be absolutely great!*). However, no matter where one decides to begin their journey (*on long straight roads or not*) one will still be on the great and hopefully enjoyable squircular road of life and all it has to offer.

26

The Round Table knights knew that a circle (*or a squircle*) could create a feeling of equality and respect, with love being the cornerstone. Just as the great creator of all beings may have thought, when the creation of this squircular world may have been created from a simple tiny but squircular spot. If we are all true share-olo-gists and we become "share aware", we can all be equal in our freedom, hope, faith, thoughts, lives, loves, ambitions and spirit, which is what we all should be and hopefully may be, forever the cause of.

Yucckie and Mahzie, when faced with what some might call a "problem", use their great friendship, thoughts and dreamer mind-set to see a problem simply as another new door to adventure. If and when this door is opened it can take them on a journey of new solutions or inventions. The opening of this door holds the inspirational sparks that are always more than welcome when creating things that some would call "*art*". Finding an open door to collaborative creation is always an exciting time for Yucckie and Mahzie, because creating solutions & inventions with friends is amazing to them.

Some have asked, "How do these two and their friends have the funds to live this way, travelling again and again and again almost everyday"? It has been said that, It's is a well-known fact that both Yucckie and Mahzie became incredibly wealthy, wise and quite healthy from the creation of their "Harmless but Helpful" fun inventions business. This is why they never have to consider finding funding for their life's travels, living in the best locations, eating the finest foods and never wanting for anything, other than more great friends and more great experiences. This is something you will learn as this story (*with your page-turning assistance*) further unfolds.

With all of their extra funds, they as a team, decided to assist all people by passing on the great knowledge of how everyone is an "I can", and never an "I can-not". So onward they went with their company slogan of "Harmless and Helpful" and the creation of their fun inventions. They always keep & kept to the simple company philosophy that even the smallest of solutions could create a good and great change for everyone on this great earth, or even the ever-expanding and infinite u-ni-verse. Yucckie and Mahzie double- mindedly invented amazing things, like the "Bananasaurus" car air-freshener system (*"Guaranteed to freshen the air in your car in the most eco-friendly way". You've gotta love those bananas — good for the body and the smell in your car!*). Can you handle it was quite awesome as it was an adjustable handle for everything that needed a handle, but had none at all.

One of their more obvious ideas for a "Harmless but Helpful" prevention inventions, came to both Yucckie and Mahzie at exactly the same moment, but when they were in two different locations! Both walked through the door of their different homes and were told it was their turn to vacuum the house. At that moment, *Kablamo Krazamoh!* A synchronized epiphany happened to both! Why would anyone spend so much time vacuuming every room in the house, which mostly needed vacuuming because of the dog losing or shedding its winter coat. All you really have to do is vacuum the source, which is the big hairy dog, of course! So fix it they did, by creating a doggie-door vacuuming thingamabobicle that saved them time and even gave the dog, when it passed through, a Swedish deep-tissue massage! How do they do it!?

I even once caught wind of a story about how Yucckie and Mahzie created a way to grow square potatoes, saving space in all of the world's supermarkets and cupboards while even providing solutions for spaceships travelling out of this world. Just the idea of square potatoes is incredible! In fact, Yucckie and Mahzie also heard, after taking a trip to NASA, that one of the biggest challenges for space travel is how to store food! I'm quite sure that trip to NASA was the main motivation to focusing on the idea of reshaping food, naturally and organically of course, taking no

GMO's to Mars!

Being a mathematical music creator and lover, Mahzie's best-selling gadget is one he calls 'Theme Song'. Theme song was and is a soft, speaker-filled necklace that plays your chosen theme songs at any time & any place to help keep your confidence up (*and keep us dancing & rocking, like the stars that we all are*!). Mahzie likes to share his music with all, but if it becomes too loud he can adjust his theme song device, so that only he can hear the music and all of the other great, joy-filled, fun beats and sounds. He certainly doesn't want to bug anyone who doesn't want to partake in his musical fun, beats and sounds.

This highly magnetic and creative duo, much later on in their lives, formulated and created a global chain of refill stores, so nobody ever needed to buy a plastic container or bottle (*except for the first one of course*!). With the creation of refill stations, there are now no extra bottles or containers on the streets, floating in the oceans, or left in the parks for anyone to cry about or shout any "ahrrrrrg's", or even for small animals to choke on or up-chuck or even barf. Those poor little animals and their plastic rubbish-caused scars! Yucckie and Mahzie were hoping, with this new, global refill system, that the world's toxic rubbish problem would be all but gone and gratefully left in ancient stories and folklore.

Clever is also what these two are, which could be another reason for their humongous happy hearts. Yucckie and Mahzie are so truly cool smart, they've even social media-ly connected with some of the world's greatest companies & leaders in an effort to create solutions for all of the current issues of the world, just and simply, for a start. They've met with; Children's Hospitalians, Healthy Blackmore-ians, Planet Arkians, Apple Mac users, Dell laptop-ers Masekala-ians, Vissler-ians, Study-groupers, Mathematians, Governmentarians, Gourmet Garden-ians, Coastal-watchers, Coastal Alliances, Yogis and Yogettes, Surfrider Foundation-ers, the French, Americans, Australians, Africans, Russians, the Japanese, the Chinese, Belgians, Mexicans, Canadians, the Swiss, South Americans, Pacific Islanders, Icelandians, Norwegians, Swedes, Finns, Antarcticans, Plastic Paradisians, Western Unioners, Seventh Sky-ers, Google-ers, Yahoo-ers, Skype-ers, Linkedin innovators, Harlem Hospitilians, Universitarians, Fox-tel-ers, musicians, Televisians, Eco-warriors, Sea Shepherd-ers, Make-a-wish foundation-ers, Scienticians, Athletes, Actors, Baptist care-givers, Pay Pal-ers, Ocean Festival goers, Cape-to-Cape explorers, David Wolfe super-food followers, Bahai-ians, Hawaiians, Grannies, Grand-pops, Mums, Poppas, and all people looking for a kinder, more caring society on our shared earthly spot. They even contacted United States President Barack

Obama and Sir Richard Branson about dust storm building solutions for people thinking about living way out on planet Mars!

Yucckie and Mahzie, along with many of their newfound friends, have solved several problems. With your help they can continue to create more solving, sharing, love and kindness for all. They are always happy to assist with problems no matter how big they are, or how small. Creating solutions and watching these solutions in action can give one a great, magical feeling of euphoria, almost like the feeling one gets from the long, surf tube-riding feeling of the "unknown zone". The unknown zone is the place for only the most faith-full of the faith-full, who trusts that there may be something greater than themselves that will help them to succeed all the way out of what may be twisty, tubing, tunnel, situations that are sometimes quite exciting, and sometimes even frightening places.

Either way, solutions for now and for the future may be up to the greater good of the you, and the me that are, and will be. All of Yucckie and Mahzie's inventions are of interest and quite unique. The Smellifier, the Sound and Smell Trilloquism_Helmet, the Vinegarated Clean cleaner, New-butts Insulation, laptop-shell-cladded-squircular-tree-pod homes, pocket-sized juicers, palm frond sunbrellas, and even large-scale solar energy magnificators that share the Sun's great energy with those who may not be able to afford to purchase this amazing technology which is used for harvesting this heavenly universal resource.

Yes, this is true — Yucckie and Mahzie love to create solutions for the many, or even one, or a few. "Any kind of helpful" is what they are excited to do or to be. Another gift this dynamic of two also share is a love of surfing, no matter if on the water, Internet, wind, mountains or streets. Different ways to ride and rate the rolling waves of riding lines is extremely attractive to the all-wave surfer in these two. This love of wave surfing also gives them a special way of being, a style of thinking, living, loving and giving. Like many things, surfing & joy have a different meaning or scale of measure for the many people of the world. Yucckie and Mahzie created a rating scale with symbols for the joy that they shared, of a 1 a 3 and a 2, and an infinite one, of course.

- *If it was a joy rating of 1, it would be equal to; !☺,*
- *If it was a joy rating of 2, it would be equal to; !!☺,*
- *If it was a joy rating of 3 it would be equal to; !!! ☺,*

If the joy goes beyond measure, the scale would be infinite and equal to; !!!!☺~. These symbols would best describe the story, moment or feeling to those that were in the know, just as you and I are now.

One of the most wonderful things about the act of surfing, for both Yucckie and Mahzie, is & are the so many different kinds of folks & heroes that one could meet and befriend while surfing. They could meet and make friends with anyone in the surf from; nurses to doctors, to plumbers and speed walkers, from builders to post-people to singers to monks, from muffin-makers, to mechanics to mountain riders, to plumbers, from astronauts to yogi's and yogettes, to students, to opticians, to skaters, to cyclists, from healers, to even those searching to be healed. Riding and sharing the ever-changing waves of the ocean has a great equalizing and therapeutic effect. All those who partake in the art of surfing have to start at the same position, of the beginning, and never truly master what may be an unknown end. With surfing you see, there is no end, only a life of endless changes and absolute infinity. All surfers equally have different experiences and rides to tell stories about, with infinitely unique descriptions for all and one to enjoy quietly, or even with a wild yelp out loud.

As with an artist's canvas, each individual has their own amazing wave-ish canvas on which to create and draw unique lines. Each day, this maze of mystical, curly, curving lines disappears as quickly as the morning dawn, never to be seen again and never to

34

be re-drawn, the artist being only "in the zone" once and leaving none of the same tracks behind. It has been said by many and a few, that owning of the zone is a timeless moment that one should experience before one's journey of life is ready for the next level, which may be that much closer to the infinite grace of The Great Spirit and the unchartered beyond-ness of me and you.

This "owned zone" that we now speak of, has been hidden behind the pathway of a bending Beckham-kicked soccer ball. This same "owned zone" can maybe be heard, on the silent slide of a Ryna Scheckler zip-slidden hand rail or even in the timeless drum beat and dance of a Native American "walking-in-time" tale. This owned zone may be witnessed in a ballet dancer's floating, graceful flight or heard in the perfect '*ping*' of a golfer's (*connected to the ball*) perfect driving swing. This 'owned zone' maybe hailed in a basket baller's slam-dunk-glide that forces a ball to swish the net as it sinks, or even in the surfing bottom-turn set-up for a Hawaiian island perfect tube ride, on a massive wave known to the world as "Pipeline"!

The owning of the zone, in wave surfing; is that incredible time-machine moment when one's actions are beyond gravity, weight, time and sound which is an effortless slide-glide. This feeling is one that everyone should, and hopefully will, someday know. This unique moment happens when one has reached a pinnacle of personal achievement, as owner of their particular zonal moment in time. For a scientifically- and philosophically-minded surfer, this moment is described as; when each and every bit of one's physical and quite math-a-magical molecules, electrons, leptons and protons are synchro-sinc-ti-ly vibrating with the waves of the great oceans, space and time making you as unbreakable as the water and as immovable as the sky.

For the non-science-minded surfer, it's heard in a bellowing, bright-hearted yelp from the deepest part of one's diaphragmatic soul, with pure and total stoke! Either way, both experiences are one and the same. This moment is in the deep grind of a tube ride, which can be louder than the roar of Niagara Falls or silent enough to put a baby to sleep. This is truly an aqua-magical mother's womb of a place. If you would be so kind, tell us *your* own story of an "owning the zone" moment, which we can all cherish in our zonal minds special space. If you haven't had this joyful moment in your life as of yet don't worry or fret, because you will … and Yucckie and Mahzie will be waiting to read the stories that you may send to us about the moment of your best.

Now that you've come this far, we will consider you another great star. We, of the Y&M squircle of friends will be your loyal friends, infinitely without any known end. All you need to do is stay in touch by email or post and Yucckie or Mahzie will respond, with special handling and care being the utmost. It's both Yucckie and Mahzie's kind ways that you'll learn, and you'll see that they'll always stay your close, honest and happy good friends, no matter how near or how far, that you may be.

Chapter 1 –Essential Fabric & Style

In the beginning, we were here together during a particularly auspicious & wonderful day, or what may be just another memory or even an imaginative figment one might say. You're friend & mine, young Yucckie was creating what he would like to hopefully happen in his future, something amazing without a doubt, on his "Solution-Visio-drawing-board"(*some call this a vision board*).

Yucckie always seemed most comfortable when in his room, surrounded by all of the wonderful things that he had collected or created during his not so long lifetime. His collections included a very interesting and obviously handmade pair of red, sort of silken, universal shorts, which he always wore along with his multi-use utility belt. This short & utility belt combination was perfect for his lifestyle as they carried all that he would actually need on a daily basis. I know what you are thinking, what about the cold days? Yucckie was always thinking ahead, and had hand crafted some zip-on legs just in those more chillious & serious of cases. This multi-use utility belt had multiple pockets and hook-able spots that could be used for so many things, such as keys, notes, coins, surf wax, a rain poncho, tiny tools, things for rock climbing, camping & even smallish pad-locks. The shorts however, were especially interesting due to the silken red fabric from which they had been hewn. This came from a much larger extremely precious stock of fabric that had been slowly scissored off, trimmed back and passed across many generations of his family, having left just enough remnant for their creation and of course with the addition of Yucckie's happily designed logo & trade mark. (!!!!☺~) = Infinite Joy.

When Yucckie was given this cloth, Yuckkie had been told that this red fabric was quite old, nearly 2000 or more years, to possibly be most close to exact. Other pieces of this cloth had been used for many things, from warming a precious newborn baby under a great star in a cave, to drying someone's water washed feet in an ancient old fashioned stable, story or fable. It was even said to have saved the lives of many a great wandering eagle. This fabric was also apparently used as a rescue flag by a vegetable clothed, fruit & fish eating man, saving his last piece of red apple, whilst shipwrecked on a desert island surrounded by a flock of thousands very literate & hungry, vegetarian seagulls! Sqwuack,

sqwuack sqwuack, squwack! Whew! What a mouthful or words that was for me to divulge, which I'm sure my grammar teacher & some others would say is highly un-evolved. Some may say these thoughts are illegal and too far "outside of the box". Why stretch one's mind or one's tongue, or maybe even their sox, if one does not have to, when it is much safer to stay in one's box?

Being that this fabric was quite special, Yucckie felt it best to keep it with him always. So this was another reason why Yucckie fashioned this amazing fabric with all of its magical thread into something that he would always have with him, even in bed. Otherwise, Yucckie's colorful mix of his family's life story thread may have been forgotten, lost, bleached or even left on a deserted island or beach.

In the time cycle washed out dilution of life's laundry load, of global "old sayings" & stories, some of the most vibrant & colorful stories have to fade and change to grow in their worth. No matter how well we color-fast guard the stories of the flag of our own lands stories & old sayings, all stories & old sayings must fade & blend to be relevant and renewed, or they will simply disappear as just another obsolete point of view.

This brings to mind the old saying that, "absence of someone or in this case something, makes the heart grow fonder." When timeless old sayings and stories are brought back to life, we may appreciate life much more and will truly be glad & revived. Such is life, without change it cannot evolve to a better form then it was before. So Yucckie made sure to fashion his fabric & his stories to adapt & to evolve. After creating his universal shorts, the extra or leftover fabric was always used to repair and update his amazing universal shorts, with new patches or re-threads and creative changes of all sorts. With his stories that he heard from his travels in life, he would learn more about their meanings, as he grew older each year, which caused and keeps causing a change in perspective for things that he saw & sees and could and can hear. These new revelations and meanings would change him and his friends, as they organically expanded his & their minds and luckily not just their heads.

Oh perish the thought some would say, but in nature all color must change or even fade away, only to return in another more unique and intriguing way. As we watch the trees change ever so subtly, day after day, we learn so much about the true speed limits meant for all life. Yucckie also knew and now knows that life is organic, in the way that it moves & grooves naturally as the seasons and as all water must flow.

To Yucckie, the threads of this beautiful red fabric were the linkage thread that was his story lifeline to many interesting thoughts of the past, present and perhaps even of the future. So he wanted to keep it close by and keep it close by is what he did. These were truly amazing universal shorts or at least that's what they became for him. These shorts could be used for just about anything that the world could throw at them. These shorts could be worn in the surf for surfing of course, hot, dry or wet weather, in space or arctic snow. In fact they could be worn anywhere that Yucckie could, or imagine, to be or to go!

In Yucckie's amazing room, there is always a minimum of at least one fish style surfboard, with a maximum of three. Each surfboard was crafted with not so normal surfboard materials of that or this particular day. These surfboards were usually made of some kind of more super, more special recyclable materials that he'd found or someone had created along the way. Somehow the special characteristics of the fish-surfboard gave him what he called a fish-vantage (secret *advantage of surfing on a fish shaped surfboard*) and allowed him to surf so many different and quite elusive kinds of waves. Each of these and his other surfboards were outfitted with a Kelly Slater or a Slater brothers leg rope, with double swivels and a hide a key pocket, to hide his key or some wax of course, of course of course!

Yucckie always gifted his surfboards with a name & for some unknown reason he always made sure to have not one, not two, but like we have said, a trilogy of three. One was called the BLT, which was a great all rounder that could handle many surf conditions. I think that he once said that the name meant that it was for 'Big, little or tall' wave conditions which were around most of all? The second of this triad was the "Club sandwich" (*rarely ridden unless the waves were massive, mostly for display only*) this board had one real purpose. The airbrush artwork, looked really cool leaning or hanging on anyone's wall.

But if the surf was especially enormous this board would then be taken down, dusted off and held with a prayer in mind just before it was paddled out into surfing conditions of which may become it's last moments of opti-mystical big wave rides. This boards artwork was powerfully visual and inspirational. It was a thought-provoking piece of art that was meant to cause feelings of confidence, love and joy for one's self and for all, while witnessing what might be this board and it's rider's last glorious paddle out.

The third surfboard was his favorite, only because it always caused quite a parking lot fuss. "The Flying Saucer", was quite small & quite wide, so much so that everyone just had to take a look at it and always asked for a ride. The flying saucer surfboard, Ohhh how smooth across the glassy waves, did it glide. It was better than even if one could imagine an ancient "Aladdin" magic carpet ride. It worked great in the mid-sized waves and even the micro-small, but best of all it fit in the boot of any small car. This board was easily carried on any beach bus and because of its width, when it was carried, it made his arms look even stronger, which is always a plus. Yes, his surfboards were all truly great and without too much fluff. Yucckie was practical you see, well too himself. Outside of the odd club sandwich, he was practical enough even for the you and I, that is really a, we.

Yucckie of course, also had a special waterproof camera to capture his memories at all kinds of different angles and funny places where one could live, laugh or play. Yucckie even used it in school to help him repeat what he had learned in class for the day. Yucckie really liked learning and loved to be smart. Math was one of his favorite subjects, although he was also quite excited about music, literature and art also!

With surfing on their minds and knowing they always had to be prepared if the surf happened to turn on, both Yucckie & his best friend Mahzie always (*yes always*) had handy a clean & ready fresh bar of "Cream" surfing wax. This special surfing wax was made in Australia and it had a special sort of proper stickiness, which had made it known to be the best wax around. This cool surfing wax could always be found in their pre packed & prepped small travel kit which was prepared & filled with; Fin key's, ding repair, sunscreen & other quick fixing things they needed just in case of something (*surf-wise*) needing to be repaired after breaking down. Both Yucckie & Mahzie carried this philosophy of 'practical preparation' beyond surfing and were always prepared with things that were needed for daily adventures to be had. They always carefully shared these surf travel kit items and kept them organized, maintained and close at hand to be easily located or found.

Chapter 2 – Fish Faith

Yucckie always seemed to make things in the most nature reflective way. Yucckie would shape all that he could build to mimic the natural world in only the most respectable and curvaceous of ways. Mahzie was more of a mathematically inclined, urban creator that loved the use of electronics & straight lines. Mahzie loved Yucckie's self created things, as long as they were In-te-gratable and comp-u-tatable with the most ethically, logically standardized, controllable space & time in mind.

Mahzie would use meticulous, detailed mathematical solutions to create ways to clip small inter-changeable solar panels on everything, including his jackets and hats. Mahzie believed and believes, that mathematical formulas and equations always kept and keep him on a clear path to finding what he called "math-a-magical" ways to use only the power that he needed most sus-tain-ably. In fact Mahzie was so excited about mathematics that he had hand written his favorite formulas on his wristbands, underwear and even on his sox. Mahzie's creations must always be quite modernly perfect & sustainably pure. Solar energy, recycling & global conservation were always at the very top of Mahzie's earth-eco- friendly, thoughtful, fish shaped, daily mind-mapping chart. Yucckie once made a fish shaped, mind-mapping-chart frame for a present for Mahzie out of an old piece of camphor wood that someone had thrown away. So of course being a good friend & mate, Mahzie put it to good use day after week, after day.

(First drawing of the fish shaped mind mapping chart frame)

Another interesting fact about Yucckie and his self-stylized equipment that you will see is that many things had the shape or even resembled a fish of all things. That's right, I'll say it again "a fish of all things" if heard by your ear with his voice, it would have an eloquent and kind sounding ring. Yucckie lived by a simple natural rule, which seemed great for most. Yucckie's rule was as follows; for all things he created, to be really good, they must have a reflection of nature, to have just the right balance or the perfect shapely blend. Being squircular, which as far as shapes go, a "squircle" is Yucckie's favorite one to use or to show. I think he even named his dog squircles because of his roundish, white eye-patch, as well as the squircle brown patch on his right and left paws.

Yucckie was also once taught, by a great mentor and friend, that if he learned to be a catcher of fish, he would forever be fed. Yucckie would also be able to teach others how to stay fed, and so on, and so on, infinitely, with never an end. So surrounded by fish he thought would be best, and with a head full of fish knowledge he would surely be blessed. Surrounding himself with fish and taking many fish tests would help him to know them much better, and better, and better at best.

Yucckie would become a great catcher-man for sure, if he knew all that they could do and all that they were. If this worked for him he would then show Mahzie and then many, many, many... more. Yucckie made sure to have a fish for a surfboard, a fish for a snowboard, and fish shaped skateboard, a fish shaped golf putter, tennis racket, kite, ukulele and even some other things that nobody knows what he had been thinking, or what the heck they were for. Yucckie nonetheless always opti-mystically had a vision of greatness & somehow knew just what these other things could & would become for sure.

48

Fish-surfboard

Yucckie & Mahzie as you may or may not now know, could make anything out of almost everything. I'm quite sure they created something new with something old each & everyday so they were truly never bored. If ever Yucckie or his friends came close to being bored, and the weather outside kept them inside, they played a fun game that a grand pop had invented which included a foamy, squircular thing and a special 'Y&M' scoreboard. This game you will find may just be the first ever invented Olympic rain sport! In fact he was once heard to say, "If any person can make something, then I can maybe make that something or something like it. If I learn & I try & I learn & I do I will make that thing and probably even something incredibly fun and maybe never thought of before, which would be absolutely brand new!

One of both Yucckie & Mahzie's shared great non-living heroes was a fellow by the name of Benjamin Franklin. Benjamin was a man of great optimism, great inventions & plans for the future of things, which is why they liked his story so much. If you Google Benjamin Franklin, you may come to like him as well and as such. Yucckie & Mahzie were inspired by Benjamin Franklin, which helped them to live by another interesting rule that was something like this; "There were no real great walls that could stop a free thinking minds path". One just has to simply learn and do the math, create a plan and then just actually commit, and then of course do whatever the task".

That's right, they also knew that good old "Pythagoras" (*another one of their non-living heroes*) was right about the magic & power of mathematics. If you don't know about Pythagoras or even about Ben Franklin it's Ok, there is still plenty of time to learn about them. You will see that with mathematics, even the greatest of walls can be overcome quite easily, just about anywhere, by just about anyone. With mathematics, anyone could find ways over or around any wall that would enclose or surround. If one was to study the magic of mathematics or the physics of lifting off, climbing over, or even silently tunneling under the ground, one could create solutions to even inventing a flying skate-snow or surfboard that levitates effortlessly without even the slightest of sounds. Hmm, could this be the long awaited hover-board invention finally coming around?

Ask any bird and they will tell you of flying and how. The difficulty with birds is, study you must their language for along patient spell. Then sing this language proud and out loud and hope that you learned it well. Nobody else will know what you've sung, but the flock of millions of birds that will be coming to be fed, until they are done. So make sure that you have many crusts of bread, in your hands, or you may be feeling "too bad & so sad", said someone's brother named Daniel to me, once in a way that I may never ever forget.

I am always grateful for such comments that survive timelessness tests. But to find a bird language instructor may also be tough and as unnerving as that last paragraph that you just read. Before we fly we must begin with simple math or logic. With our mind in the sky, but our feet safely planted on the ground, or with a safety harness, a helmet and some good knee, elbow pads, or many soft pillows all around on the ground.

Chapter 3 – Life Keys for You & Me

Yucckie and Mahzie always suggest mathematics as being the most logical language to learn, as it is the basis of every great foundation that one could create, that surely will stay solid and firm. Why, without mathematics we have no surfboards, skateboards, body boards, music, snowboards, X-games or motor cross jumps. Without mathematics we have no airplanes, cookies, I-pads, bridges, doctors, skate parks or "Go Pro" cameras for filming the bumps or the lumps. Without mathematics we would have no perfect handrails, Tesla's free energy, space shuttles, fun boxes or even a birthday cake & escargot snails. Without mathematics we wouldn't have kite boards, Arctic Challenges, the Olympics, the Mt. Baker banked slalom, Paige Alms' big wave surfing, the Bob Burnquist backyard skate park, or corrected sunglass lenses, Sally Pearson's surprise finishes & starts. Without mathematics we wouldn't have motorized back flips by Carey Hart. Without mathematics we wouldn't have cool smart musicians like Lead Belly, TobyMac, Jack Johnson, Renny Field, Paula Fuga, Plum, Xavier Rudd, Woody Guthrie, Ziggy Marley, Michael

Franti, Stevie Wonder, the Ventures, Pink or even funny things like a finger board to finger-skate in the tub or the sink. With out mathematics, we wouldn't even have that running loop-da-loop, that a man called Damien Walters ran by running at speeds of eight kilometers per hour, I think? There are so many things that we can do with mathematical problem solving solutions. Math even holds the keys to solve air, water, noise, space and even some kinds of fashion pollution.

With the joyful knowledge of mathematics, Yucckie & Mahzie's most favorite show & tune in 1936 was created, sung & drawn for the entertainment of the me's and the you's and can still be watched on you-tube. To be remembered forever long. This favorite song & animated show was called & came to be known as, "I love to Singa" by none other than Owl Jolson, who's life love was simply about singing one great and simple song. Why just the other day, or was it long ago, it doesn't really matter when, but here anyway it goes. Yucckie & Mahzie were on their own world tour where they witnessed a great skateboarder by the name of 'Danny Way' jump over what was thought of in China, and by the rest of the world, to be the greatest wall of them all.

Using mathematics and a big brave heart of course, is how this great wall of a problem, by a young skateboarder, was easily and finally solved! Speaking of great massive walls, they had even eye-witnessed on other great Y&M math-a-magical, mystical tours, some great sports athletes & other kinds of heroes including the likes of; Mark Healey, Greg Long, Dave Wassel, Makua Rothman, Talon Clemow, Shane Dorian, Dave Mira, Carey Hart, Guillome Morrisette, Kelly Slater, Taj Burrow, Bede Durbrige, Nathan Fletcher, Bruce & Andy Irons, Paige Alms, Tom Carroll, Mark Richards, Tom Curren, Terje Haakonsen, Anne Molin Kongsgaard, Gerry Lopez, Stephanie Gilmore, Toby Mossop, Michael Peterson, Barney Miller, Layne Beachley, Angela Sun, Bethany Hamilton, Parko, Jordy, Cordy, Damien & CJ Hobgood, Kai Otton, JJ Tomas, Gigi Ruff, Dane Reynolds, Dean Morrison, Nicolas Muller, Kelly Clark, Gene Hardy, Daniel Jones, Adriano De souza, Sophia Mulanovich, Silvana Lima, Kim Mearig, Juli Shulz, Peg + Cat, Todd Chesser, Greg Wilson, Kassia Meador, Shaun White, Mick Fanning, Sammy Luebke, Ingemar Backman, Tony Hawk, John John Florence, Barton Lynch, Wayne Lynch, Ross Powers, Craig Kelly, Bucky Lasek, Stevie Caballero, Eddie Rategui, Steve Saiz, Christian Hosoi, Rob Machado, Bradley Gerlach, Jeff & Billy Anderson, Garrett McNamara, Kobe Abberton, Danny Davis, Jamil Khan, Jodie Downs, Keir Dillon, Jodie Cooper, David Benedek, Ron Ziebell, Jim Rohn, Zig Ziglar, Hannah Teeter, Stefan Gimpl, Heikki Sorsa, Barrett Christy, Rainos Hayes, Eero Ettala, Eero

Niemala, Lauri Heiskari, Kazuhiro Kokubo, Kjersti Buass, Steve Fontes, Shayne Pospisil, Jesse Billauer, Co Co, Micheal & Mason Ho, Curtis Ciszek, Sammy Luebke, Gretchen Bleiler, Kelly Clark, Dustin Barca, Jamie Andersen, Danny Kass, Jim Rippey, E.B. White, Russell Winfield, Bjorn & Erik Leines, Layne Beachley, Torah bright, Martin Chernik, Travis Rice and so many more that conquered some of the most incredible feats of infamy with an effortless mastery that so many others have never even known to be, or have never seen before.

Some of these amazing moments in time were even missed by some of the greatest filmers & photographers like; Doctor Zapalac, Jon Foster, Tim Bonython, Anthony Pearse, Scotty Needham, Pierre Wikberg, Dave Seaone, Ari Marcopoulos, Taylor Steele, Simon "Shagga" Siffigna, Iwa, Poli or the Dawg known as the Mac. No matter how wide they're widest of wide angle, fish or red-eye lenses were expanded; they were unable to capture all of these moments without connecting to a global satellite all at the same time. So, lucky were Yucckie and Mahzie, to have been there and to have been witness to most of these wonderful real life adventure moments of greatness!

Yucckie & Mahzie even witnessed a man called David Beckham overcome a great so-called challenge of a wall, by finding his way to the bending of the direction of a quite standard soccer-ball, or what some called telepathically changing the trajectory of a foot-kicked round-ball. It was, and is only because Yucckie & Mahzie made it a point of showing up for all of these moments and chasing the feeling of being "Crispy like-a-biscuit" that this became true. This Crispy like-a-biscuit feeling, is one, which is when you are so tired from having a great time at whatever you've been doing all day, that you could just about crumble up anywhere and fall asleep with a massive biscuit eating smile on your face. Ha ha and a hearty ho ho! & LOL (*laugh out loud*) is all I can say as well as a speed texted R-O-T-F-L (*roll on the floor laughing*) for those that are instant messaging today!

Yucckie & Mahzie had once been told, that "90% of success in life is about being present". With this information, Yucckie & Mahzie did their best to do just that, and be active participants in as much of life, and all the moving & still moments of creation that were (*and some that were not*) of interest to them. This was far beyond the area that was originally thought to have been in the possible plan for them. Many imagined that this duo would never accomplish much or go so far in this modern world. But, both Yucckie and Mahzie used their active imaginations to create a clear path to get them to where many have said they would

56

have liked to have been, to have shared in the great laughs, joy and experiences that life can offer to all. "Where there is a will there is also a way" for you & for me, with togetherness in mind is known as the "We".

In Yucckie's most amazing bedroom, as he did with many of the blank spaces that were placed in his path, were Yuckkie's trail of happiness drawings, which for some created such a great printed path. Wherever he had been, Yucckie created hand drawn (*with colored chalk or sometimes in beach sand, so they weren't permanent because Yucckie knew that his style would change and so should the look of this trail of happiness*) hearts & smiles representing friend's known and friends that he may someday wish to have. Perhaps this would be his only left behind legacy, but somehow I think maybe more fun for all, may be his story that will be remembered the most.

In one corner of his mostly squircular room was one well-loved & worn wooden skateboard, with lots of other smiley faced objects of worldly origins too. A short stocky, wooden box radio that he and his grand-pop had hand built a long time before, which ironically just happened to be sitting next to his very modern, ultra clean touchscreen computer sitting with honor & great stability on a perfect stack of old but clean shoe-boxes at the perfect standing

57

level on the uneven wooden floor. Next to this stack of shoe-boxes was also a peculiar little locked wooden box that was given to him by his great, great, great grand parents, which had never been opened, as he had never had a key for the lock. Yucckie kept this locked small wooden box, for the sake of his family tree. Yucckie even owned a much used, worn and loved indo ball & board" for great balance & stability practice, of course.

Yuckkie's computer & I-phone was well equipped with a Wi-Fi & wireless connection, all the key app's (*applications*), software & programs, and even Skype, Viber, & Zarfo which would allow him to communicate to the world in as many languages that he could ever imagine or even believe to be used or behold. These great modern machines of unspeakable ease also came with all of the searching engine access that any human could ever need! Googles, Yahoos & Bings, to both Yucckie and Mahzie were such great and informative searching & ingenious things. Grateful they were and they are to the Bill Gates' and Steve Jobs' and all of they're other knowledge-tool creative rock stars.

Education was prime and important, no matter where they could get it. Education was their foundation for their inevitable solution filled futures for sure! Yuckkie & Mahzie both knew that when they had computer or smart-phone access, they could learn almost anything, at a moment's notice, with a flick of a switch or just a touch on the screen. They used these great electronic tools to fill so many needs, yes indeed. I think I may have even heard about educational resources like, Mooks and Coursera from either Yucckie or Mahzie. They were onto things before most, but shared with one, and with all, from the mountains to the valleys and from coasts to coasts.

Yucckie & Mahzie had & have an undying love for the You & Me or otherwise known as "the we". To them, they always do their best to think in terms of "We" as it is a truly important way to live and to be. They are aware that there are so many people alone in their lives. But being alone or lonely can be easily overcome, if all of us just made a few more new friends, just one or two more times. This duo believes that one should be aware, that one can never have too many friends, but without even one friend, one would be quite lonely. So together we must all make more friends.

Up to this point, if you have any great questions or if there is an answer that you seek, please don't hesitate to ask your new friends, Yucckie & Mahzie.

Yucckie@yucckie.com or **Mahzie@yucckie.com**

Yucckie.com

60

Chapter 4- A Gift For You

This is a special page made just for you as our new friend in our crew! Tear-out or print this page and always keep it in your pocket or somewhere safe. It is our gift to all of our friends who wish to feel forever good and sometimes even great. With only good intentions in mind, say this to yourself daily, at least 3 or more times. Say this for no less than thirty days, with no maximum, so this will become yours forever. Then give these magic words as a gift to someone else someday as a friend.

- *I am truly amazing, I am brilliant & I am strong.*
- *I can do anything that I put my mind to as long as it is honest, good and not wrong.*
- *I love myself & I love everyone else.*
- *I am grateful, thankful & kind.*
- *I am humble.*
- *I am truly amazing. Thank you.*

To remember and use these simple words with gratitude is always wise & to know that YATA (*you are truly amazing*) when speaking to another, or IATA (*I am truly amazing*), when speaking to yourself), if believed is always true & cannot be taken by anyone, from you.

It is a simple fact that "You are truly amazing", as you are a perfect and forever changing version of you. There is no better you, than the one that is you. You are so truly amazing that you may be the first to create a world changing idea that may feed the world's hungry & fix crooked spines. Or even change the way we surf, snowboard, skate or rock & mountain climb. You are so amazing that with a simple "random act of kindness" made by you (*with the magic of IATA in mind*); like a smile from your face given to some one else's frowning face, will give them a new found joy taste, that could one day even help that person become an astronaut on their way to saving people in need, all the way out in outer space!

Yucckie and Mahzie have always believed that only love from people that know that they are amazing can save the world. First we must all know what love is, or at least agree upon a common definition for love. For some, this isn't so simple even though others say that it is. At a minimum, we should all be able to agree to disagree on what love truly is. What is it you say? Hopefully the stories that follow will reveal what it is for Yucckie and Mahzie.

We will surely know more when the great mystery is revealed … or maybe we will never know much of anything. But if & when you become aware of your amazingness, this will be the beginning of good and great changes in the world, for all connected beings.

Chapter 5 –Then & Now

Yucckie was blessed with a respect & love for the old & for the new. He was also quite lucky to have been bestowed a collection of beautiful cared for big books in his room that were passed down from his granny & grand-pop. These books (*known as encyclopedias*) with their word-full pages helped him to learn about all of the wonderful things that the world & universe has had to offer, far before computers came along for the ease of me & for you. This always created a big question for Yuckkie, as he thought, "where should I learn from today"? Shall I learn from my school lessons? Shall I learn from my computer, or my books? Each taught in very different and unique ways. Yucckie thought both books and computers (*electronic tablets included*) feel and felt so different, as one could never really curl up in a warm bed to fall asleep with a computer, as it was too mechanically frigid. However, the fore-mentioned problem was solved the day Yucckie and Mahzie (*with the magic of IATA in mind*), co-invented their comp-uto-pillow with 3D pages that seemed to jump off of the screen and turned so beyond book-like, with such similarity, that Yucckie almost had a night of sweating his bed! It could be too much of a good thing. That is a-whole-nother lions tale that you may come to know in due course, but lets get on with this show far beyond that source. One could quite easily curl up and sleep with just about any book or even with a few. Just another dinner fork in the road of life, is what Yuckkie said, with a great unanswerable sigh, a breath that came from deep in his belly, to be fully exhaled, so none in his throat would be caught. He may find an answer to this quandary one day in his dreamtime mind, he thought.

His bedroom was ever so interesting, especially when one took a really close look. You would have noticed something other than just a fishing pole or a fishing hook. Like the hand made & polished, antique box radio sitting honorably & proudly just next to the clean, silver apple computer, also a hand held 'GPS' unit next to a well-worn-out army compass that looked quite worldly, used & by many hands touched. There, upon his chest of drawers sat a beautifully hand crafted steel, belt driven sewing machine along side a polished aluminium & plastic I-phone. This I-phone, was curiously perched on top of a vintage phonograph player, which was so much more proud & astute, with its amazing warm wooden & polished brass curves. I never could quite figure that one out.

Both played such beautiful sounding music, with their antique & modern electrical ways. When it came down to the choice, the phonograph player always seemed to come first. Maybe this was an effect of his friendly relationship, fun & fond memories he had of the time spent with his granny & grand pop.

Yuckkie remembered taking many a great adventure with his granny & grand pop, who used to take him rummaging through all of the local salvage & opportunity shops. These Op shops, seemed like bank vaults or time capsules of all of the old misty & magical days. It sometimes felt like being a great time traveller who was guided by them, guided at least some of the way. This is surely what created his love, affinity and respect for the antiquities & gadgets of older days. Yucckie felt that things made back then always had quite amazing curvicular-styling and interestingly what seemed to be more heart-warming designer ways. For when you put the handcrafted curves and materials of the olden days the modern designers marriage to modern efficiencies are exposed as simply being made for those things that are said to be most needed by many people today. To Yucckie the past was not better nor worse just different in so many obviously temperate ways.

Yuckkie's granny & grand-pop thought that by taking Yuckkie on these great op-shop adventures, that it would be a nice way to teach Yuckkie about the history and the value of things from their life-times. Granny & Grand pop's lifetimes have sometimes been called by most of people, quite sadly & disrespectfully as the "olden days". One of Yucckie's secret & most favorite things to do, would be to sometimes just sit in the middle of a group of grannies & grand- pops and quietly listen to all of their amazing stories & wise advice of what to not, and what to do. One great piece of advice that always stood quite tall was simply, to be kind, honest and respectful and once true love was found, one was to never stop "courting the one that you love".

He didn't really know what all of these words, stories and sayings meant, but he knew that they would make sense and be invaluable knowledge as his life time was being spent. He (*with the magic of IATA in mind*), would also sometimes imagine himself & what his next great adventure would be like, now that his mind was so full of so many re-plantable great seeds of wisdom to utilize, explore and enjoy. Another answer to the reason for Yucckie's searching & adventurous ways, may have been Yuckkie's secret search for the rest of the amazing red silken fabric who's qualities as well as the story of its origins are another long lion's tale that you may learn of some how, some where, some day on another **Y&M** math-a-magical mystical tour, (*Y&M mmt*) one may say.

No matter what, Yuckkie & Mahzie simply liked to make things that would last for a very along time, just as the now "antiquities" from the golden era of his granny & grand dad's days & just like stories of their wonderful & adventurous ways. I'm not sure if I've mentioned this, but Yucckie & Mahzie had special names for those type of "been here longer folks" that they met on life's many roads. Those "been here longer folks", the ones that most people would call "OLD" because of their age in years, who were due much respect, love, kindness and not to live in fear. In fact, Yucckie & Mahzie thought those grannie or grand-pop aged folks were so incredibly amazing! These special kinds of people were great holders, handlers & gift givers of treasure troves of wisdom that was timeless & never ever to be called, used up or old.

(Yucckie & Mahzie called these more time blessed people; "Diamond Eyed Wisdom Keepers" or D.e.w.ks for the men & Duchess' for the ladies).

When listened to patiently, their stories when gifted and told to them were always thought of as some of the greatest of lucky treasures. One must simply listen & hear with ones open mind & heart because this is where one can truly become wise & also quite smart.

If you looked into the eyes of one of these great wisdom gift givers, one would be graced with the light of what seemed to be star sparkly bright diamonds. With just one glance you could easily feel & believe in the jewels of their wisdom, oddly enough without even having to hear them speak. Being in the presence of one of these amazing people was also like being in a warming embrace of the wings of a great guardian angel. Even the physically smallest and most seemingly frail one of them all would give you a unique sort of comfort. In these great listening moments you & I or the "we", all could learn & be pleased.

I am comforted in knowing that Yucckie & Mahzie care enough to search for and discover so many things that may have otherwise been forgotten and lost in an overflowing, robotically cold, data-collection-focused, technological sea. It's not nice when things go missing in the lost land of "E", or the place known as "Electronica" to Yucckie and Mahzie. Electronica it seems is like a black hole, as it sucks up random emails, txt messages and other

71

things that disappear into who knows where? Maybe we will find out where all of our lost messages have gone some day soon or maybe we will not.

Yucckie & Mahzie would learn about cursive handwriting & posting letters through the mail system (*not just on Chat room & Facebook walls*) writing incredible letters & the magic that they could create. This magic had a much warmer feeling & much better than a txt, email or Tweet. This magical power that should still always be used & not given up, because it can love a lonely soul in a patient and more long lasting way, that an electronic-robotic-messaging society should never ever put down or negate. There are still plenty of folks who need to be loved in this kind and patient way. Why even a hug, a door knock or a simple handshake is becoming a lost art in a world that has been focused on the "I & electronic me". This world clearly needs to be more of a world that is focused on the "We's" that is consequently the inevitable peaceful togetherness of the you and the me! No more battles or wars over words, the way to eat eggs or cheese or the bees & the birds. At minimum, just agreeing to disagree can be ok, and living together peacefully quite happily each and every day.

Yucckie & Mahzie both are always and forever all about the art of "We". This dynamic duo of sorts enjoys bringing people of all walks & cultures together as a happy-family-world. Yucckie & Mahzie even made & make time to learn the Cherokee alphabet, some Australian aboriginal words & some ditz and dahs of Samuel Morse's code. Learning these more time-blessed languages was & is done in an effort to begin to understand, that which is, and that which was that. Both Yucckie & Mahzie believe that, there is always so much to be learned for the future, from the past.

Before & during every journey or adventure to be taken, Yucckie & Mahzie were always sure to meet with as many D.e.w.k's & for the ladies respectfully the Duchess'. These acronyms for names were befitting and right as they were uplifting & respectable code names. Each DEWK and Duchess seemed to happily enjoy them much more than using a word such as old. "More blessed" is also a better pair of words they used to describe, those respectable folks that have been here a bit longer than the younger ones of you, I or me.

Yucckie & Mahzie never liked it when people were called things that may offend or even unknowingly bring someone's spirit down. They would much rather use words to uplift a spirit and to help to bring another ones feelings up, so that they would feel great about their work & evidently quite self confident and proud. So, if you could be so kind as to remember these words; (*"Help all people feel good about themselves, as it is all of our job and our life-long responsibility"*). Yucckie & Mahzie and even the you & I that is "We", do steadily implore you to ask anyone of that "D.E.W.K or Duchess" type style or age to take the time to tell you all of their great stories of the wonderful & "great or golden-days". Bring with you your patience & a comfortable seat & maybe your best friends. Happily, it may take a while, but you definitely will want to hear all the treasure-full information that these amazing folks have to speak.

The modern things that Yucckie had or collected was some of his doing and perhaps some inspired by the pressure of his peers. So he was quite weary about surrounding himself with peers of qualified good years. So many other things in his life were quite possibly there because he was always listening to the great advice of his Mum, Dad & teachers. They were cut of the same fabric, folk tales, and adventures that most good grand folks, parents, elders and teachers are made from as well. Sometimes, Yuckkie would even collect tools at opportunity shops. For some reason to him they just seemed to feel better in his hands and in his mind, knowing that someone else had used them to fix things with love for such along time. Tools that were tested in his mind surely would work well, not hopefully, but for sure, which to him seemed quite swell. There was always something about a nice worn in handle of a hammer, spanner or screwdriver that had just the right, honest, comfortable feel in the palms of his hands, but new tools were also welcome of-course.

Yuckkie in his own op-shop searches would also find amazing vintage fabrics. These vintage fabrics were possibly created for many past kings & or queens, that when sewn on his sewing machine (*with the magic of IATA in mind*), could be fashioned into clothing of great interest, that no one of his age had ever seen. All those that did see his mastery of finished garments, would always comment on how great they are & were. They would say things like; " where did you get such amazing clothing, are they from here or are they from a far"? They all seemed to think that Yuckkie's parents were buying him new things from all of their great adventures around the world. In the reality of this fiction, Yuckkie was just buying old clothing and interesting fabrics for next to nothing and re-creating them on his great aunt Essie's antique steel belted sewing machine, all-by-himself, much like some folks did before they became our current rock-stars.

Yuckkie found unique things at the opportunity shops for almost 1/100th of the normal price. What a bargain! Yucckie thought, at least once, twice or maybe even thrice. Yucckie also knew that when he paid for things in these shops his dollars were going to good use. Most of Yucckie's dollars that were spent in op-shops, were used for the homeless in need of housing, food for empty bellied children, or helping others that may need assistance, sometimes just for a couple or often, even the multitudes. Yucckie always felt that through his op-shopping, he was also assisting many a good cause. It is also well-known fact that Yucckie made & makes sure to give much of his millions to the many people that may be in need of education, homes, assistance or even funding for creating global cures.

Some of Yucckie's best treasure-filled-finds, were the days when his granny & grand pop, like many folks in the surrounding neighborhoods would do a big spring cleaning and take all the things that they thought that they couldn't use, or someone else thought that they wouldn't use and packed it all up and took it to the tip or to the county dump, which also had an op-shop. These shops at the city tip or dump were like a massive treasure mine for this young boy endowed with such an amazing creative, wise and inventive spirit. Those Tip & Dump op-shop days (*TDo's days*) caused his little warm heart to really have a go and pump, thump & pump with joy! We have all heard the old adage, "one man's trash is another man's treasure", and in this case for Yuckkie & Mahzie all they ever saw in these sorts of places was an opportunity to create something not old, but amazingly new. So (*with the magic of IATA in mind*), amazingly new creations are what they made, which was not like many people would ever think to do today. I don't know why, it was some in-born genetic thought process, that made them think that it would be best to recycle and create something out of the old, into something new!

Everyday it seemed that young Yucckie & Mahzie were (*with IATA in mind*) always quite busy creating something really good or quite fun until they tired themselves out and fell asleep to dream of surfing, helping, skateboarding or snowboarding somewhere under the dream seeding tree or beautiful blue sky & warm embrace of the sun. Always inventing and thinking of solutions were these two, although one thing that they haven't totally figured out was another really good rain sport. I'm sure with some help from friends like you some great ideas may come about soon!!!! ☺ ~

Chapter 6 -Strange days

So as we began once before, on this not so normal day, Yuckkie's crackly wooden box radio was tuned into the weather station 103.2 Hope FM, from Sydney Australia, which he could pick-up for some reason anywhere on earth (*internet radio, I presume*). Yucckie would listen to Juli Cali or ("J.C." as they called her for short). J.C. was the only really happily optimistic weather person who possessed much more than the maximum amount of pure vocal moxy, than anyone that Yucckie had ever heard of before. On this day, the station was tuned in loud & quite amazingly clear. But during today's report J.C. sounded a bit strange, very odd & far off of her norm, which was the reporting of the usually colorful, bright sunny days and not of a torrential storm.

However after telling her radio fans about the impending storm of such horrendous magnitude, which promised heavy flash flooding, with a definite amount of extremely twirl-swirly winds that could quite possibly bend the trees & whip up the oceans into an upside down wish-washy world. An upside down wish-washy world like that of those washing machine tossing and turning nightmares of anyone's worst bed sweating nights of before. This storm would possibly be creating ocean waves so massive that even those living on Australia's great mount Warning or even California's Mammoth Mountain would take shelter far from the seashore. J.C. still gave what sounded like a semi-smile when signing off with;

"Have a nice day"? Yes...that's right, J.C. said, "have a nice day'!

After telling the listeners of this impending storm which was about to unleash its wrath all through the night into the hours of wee, "J.C." mentioned in her light, cheeky manner at the end of her forecast.

"There will be a calm & sunny next morning, so if you can sleep well, sleep tight & I would suggest please, sleep deep?!

This was of course J.C's personality. Yucckie & Mahzie always had this interesting connection with her. J.C. was quite brilliant in the way that she spoke, surfed, skated, snowboarded and how she musically walked. J.C. seemed to perfectly move and groove no matter what kind of mood that she was in. J.C. always found ways to shine, even when or if things looked as if they were coming to a sad sort of doom or gloom. J.C. would "opti-mystically" create a way for all to feel better about whatever it was that occurred, and would find a happy way to begin again and for all to have a good time. To Yucckie and Mahzie, J.C.'s ways were unique and also uncanny, sometimes they didn't know whether they should think of her as a sister, a mate, a female-twin, or just a friend. I'm sure we will one day find an answer to J.C's humble and surely quite kind origins. But, for the story of J.C. we will have to wait until the new part of their journey begins, with this story's end.

Whoo Zishkabible! Yuckkie exclaimed, I've gotta make more than sure about my questionable plight for this night. Even J.C. could be wrong, or on the other hand, maybe she could be quite right. Yucckie was one to always double check, as there may be two or sometimes three sides to every story (*what someone said, to what he had heard & what really happened with great respect for their words*). On this occasion Yucckie, being quite aware of global warming and its carbon offsetting effects. The effects seem to now be showing up as much wilder weather than most had ever seen, heard of or have known. How could Yucckie, J.C. or Mahzie, really know what to expect, or what Mother Nature was about to

80

unload. To both Yucckie & Mahzie it seemed that Mother Nature was desperately just trying to rebalance and fix the wobble in the spin of our earthly green and blue squircular home of a globe. Yucckie thought, by "Gwoahzolly Gahfookally Gosh" this storm may be bigger than what I have ever known and I would really rather not get lost, in what may be a quite massive backwash.

Being a surfer, Yucckie was aware that the giant waves may be twirled, swirled & wind blown up to, and across his highly elevated front yard! So Yucckie checked everything out. Yucckie checked all of the wave forecasts & cameras, coastal watches, magic seaweeds & Surf-lines. He checked all the weather channels that were known to him at the time. Just like the magic of a perfect math-a-magical formula it appeared that J.C's radio forecast totally checked out, and now left him no doubt! For Yucckie now knew he must be prepared for what some surfers would call a gi-normic stormy close-out!

Yucckie decided to switch on his modern silver touch screen apple computer that was stacked high on his shoe boxes on the floor, just to double, triple check with the surf report & weather on-line to see just what may be looming in the local stratosphere, mountains & even off shore! There it was, as plain as the nose on his face. There it was on his computer screen, a super-massive

81

low-pressure system just off the coast getting ready to wreak havoc upon the coastline in a matter of hours. A low-pressure system much bigger than he had ever seen! Oh my "Gahfiddy-Gah-Foodiddly-dah"! Yucckie exclaimed. So, with the magic of IATA in mind, Yucckie thought, (*just like the "coolsmart third little pig" did, in the three little pigs*) I must seal up this place & close all window & doors with much haste, as there really was no time to waste. Yucckie then thought, if I'm not prepared surely everything loose will be broken & smashed and if lightning is to strike, surely this place could be totally thrashed!

Yucckie then recalled that Mahzie had once told him a story about a massive digital swirl-twisty, blowy & magnetic, inner city, electrical windstorm. In fact when this story was told it really freaked both of them out! This swirl-twisty, windy & magnetic, inner city electric windstorm (*STW&MICEW*), which was the least of descriptions that he could say, blasted & powered through his city streets. This (*STW&MICEW*) storm changed everything that was electronic in so many & several ways, it lasted for nearly 8 weeks and four days. Mahzie recalled that after the storm had subsided and when he woke up in the morning, all that he could see for as far as he could see were some things so odd and quite strange.

82

These strange long and gangly things that he witnesses were wrapped around lamp poles, mailboxes, fire hydrants and even the smallest of leaves on small trees, in certain small city quadrants alarming to even the police. Mahzie said that this surely must have been the billions & millions of long lost black letters & numbers of txt messages and emails of some that were about business or quite personal things. These gangly numbers, letters, correct punctuations and more that fell out of the e-sky must have come back from the lost land of "E" (*Electronica*)!

I have always wondered and I'm sure you have too, what had become of all of those lost emails, txt messages, etc's, incorrect punctuations, numbers & love messages, that were thought to be gone forever. Some of which were lost by me and lost by more than just you! The clean up effort for that great storm was incredible indeed. For there had never been built a broom or vacuum machine that was able to pick-up anything that had come from the lost land of "E", of course, at least not with great ease. Sounds like another great "Prevention Invention" to be created by Yucckie & Mahzie or someone like you or like me.

With the information of this new impending wild storm, young Yuckkie (*with the magic of IATA in mind*), decided to prepare for the strongest of storm forms. With his trusty self-designed & created Yucckio-mag-matic-multi-use-tool (*YMMMUT*) in hand, Yuckkie tightened all of the screws in all of the hinges, all of the doors, all of the doors to the doors, all of the windows & the windows to the windows. He then shut and plugged up all of the places in his interesting (*what some kids may have thought that Yucckie would have had or would have been a ramshackle surf shack tree house*) built in a beautiful big & wondrous Morten bay fig tree, (*known as the dream seeding tree, or Great-gran-daddy fig tree*). You will of course learn more about great daddy fig, the dream-seeding tree, as you read further. Like most people in business today say, it is because, "We wish to be transparent and without mystery".

Yucckie's surf shack tree house was far from ramshackle. In fact this tree house was built with recycled things from modern scrap yards, tips and op-shops that he acquired or bought. Yucckie's place was not-so-ramshackle, it was more like modern art. Because of the modern scrap-waste he collected at the modern scrap yards, the materials he used to build it, were quite amazing space aged & adaptable from the finish to the start. Yucckie liked to reuse & recycle, but he also enjoyed building things to be nice, practical, long lasting & even eye pleasing.

Being the careful planner that he was, this tree house or "HQ" (*head quarters*) as it was called, was actually put together quite well and could be as weather proof as the tightest of clamshells. Yucckie's & also this shared by Mahzie's "HQ" was built with some of the greatest of throwaway technology that could be found. Yucckie & Mahzie used such amazing things for this build such as; computer shell cases and large thrown-away flat screen TV's by Samsung or Dell. They even used thrown-away jewel cases of Cd's as well. It is quite amazing what great building materials these thing became when dismantled & refurbished. They were changed & re-created into so many other great & new things, by Yucckie & Mahzie and some quite helpful friends.

The interior of this "HQ" tree house was a mirror image of Yucckie's squircular room in his parent's house. Yucckie believed, why mess with perfection, in his cheekiness to himself, as he, we and you & I do. The outside was quite another story. Yucckie gathered and separated all of the tossed away silver laptop computer shells, and some red or blue. Then in a perfect mosaic tile placement way, he created what seemed quite a space age squircular shaped room that looked quite "future fashionable" even by many design judge standards of today. This sort of judging didn't really matter to Yucckie, as he was happy with it, so that made it O.K. What a perfect shape he created, none had ever seen it before. It has been said that a squircle is quite strong. I have seen a squircular egg hold up the weight of a small car. Being that the tree house was similarly squircular, it must have been stronger than any other home shape, as it has withstood any storm that has happened so far. Yuccckie, Mahzie & I thought and think that is the case with this squircular tree house, for sure.

In his battening down of his hatches Yucckie recalled another tid-bit of wisdom that came from a "D.e.w.k or Duchess" he remembered. This tid-bit was given in the form of a most memorable loving rhyme, "A stitch in time, may truly save nine".

"A stitch in time may save nine"

These are great words that could always be used no matter how modern the times. Things quite large or quite small may one day spring a leak or let the elements in, or even worse have large holes in them. These holes that we speak of, could become big enough for your whole head to peek through. Use this advice always he did.

"A stitch in time may save nine"

86

Yucckie was a person of fine memory. He was one that listened to and used the great wisdom of the old school stories that were given to him. When it came to building any type of shelter Yucckie looked to the natural shape of hermit crabs & clamshells & tried to build anything with the ideals of the third little pig in his mind. His strategy, here was and is; if he were to build it, he would build it quite strong and build it quite well, to last many years.

Yucckie & Mahzie in their writing handbooks or on their sometimes even smarter smart phones always took great measurement & photo notes. They took notes about things that they would find while searching op-shops and even around town. These notes were quite handy for those just-in-case moments, when there was a need to be filled for a himself or herself or someone else that needed a fix-all solution to be found. Yes, whenever someone in town needed some help it seemed that they could and would always find it when they called on Yucckie or Mahzie, who because of their notes, were quite resourceful, you see. These two were always at farthest just a phone call, txt or email away.

After all of his effort, he was quite confident & happy that he did also build his 'HQ" tree house high on a hill, embraced in the lower foundation & stronger above ground roots of a very time and weather- tested, ancient & trusty Morten bay fig tree that was also considered to be Yucckie & Mahzie's dream-seeding tree friend. This dream-seeding tree friend you will learn about later in this story or now, if you contact Yucckie or Mahzie by email as well.

Both Yucckie & Mahzie believed that this great & creative little hide- away was built geo-metrically sound & planned out well enough to handle the most tremendous of mother natures storms & even some man made storms, if they were to come as well. From this central & quite amazing squircular pod dish-style place there were four similar smaller ones, in four of the higher branches for multi-directional crows nest, eagle eyed viewing of the north, east, south & west. To access the higher pods one would also stay physically fitter by climbing the natural foliage on its never ending, growth-fully changing journey chasing the sky, stars, sunrises & sunsets. If you were to stand far away enough to look at this immense dream-seeding tree, it would have looked like a giant Christmas tree decorated, Morten bay fig.

After all of this storm preparation, Yuckkie happily exclaimed, "Whew wizhoopee wow wow!" (*One of his many high falootan exclamations from who knows, where have ya?*) he then decided that he was well enough prepared for the storm & could now quite confidently go to sleep and begin to receive his most beloved dream seeds from the great branches of this great and magical dream-seeding tree. The reason that this beautiful dream-seeding-tree "HQ" (*named, Great-gran-daddy-fig-tree*) was both Yucckie & Mahzie's favorite places to go is a secret. (*LOL*) Secretly of course, Yucckie & Mahzie would always have the most wonderful and exciting dreams that would help them to create plans for new exciting adventures & prevention inventions that would always cause their active imaginations to build and to grow.

Pod-tree-home drawing

Chapter 7 – Dream Seeds

With this particular, uniquely massive, Morten Bay Fig tree, (*which Yucckie's Tree House sat in*) it was as if each of the large living leaves & branches were specifically created to collect, decipher and distribute the greatest ideas, virtues and philosophies of the universe. This wealth-filled collection would trickle down in electrical energized specs which would then be gently planted as a thought seed & a gift in the fertile minds of anyone, that may restfully & blissfully sleep beneath its magnificent canopy or its evidently quite large, comforting, covering, natural, roof-ish like lid. With all of this magic about to happen, preparation to Yucckie was the key. Just before heading off to sleep to begin receiving what he called his daily blessing of dream seeds, and of course after a belly filling "Super food" filled dinner, and a glass of cool clear water which some how always made him feel just right, Yucckie went into his nightly ritual of getting ready to receive.

First, he would get his gear off, and wrap himself in an eco-friendly organic towel. He would hang the towel on his self-styled and created recycled Yucckie hook. Then he would get straight into what he calls a "W.O.W.O" instead of a shower (*water on water off to be exact*). This "W.O.WO" is simply a really quick water saving shower. On with the water to get wet, off with the water while he soaps up, brushes his teeth, and washes his toes to his head. Then Yucckie would turn on the water to rinse off. Yucckie added it up (*did the math*) one day and found that if he did this for a full year, he could save liters & maybe even gallons of water that he had collected during the rainy season in his home made rainwater tank. Mahzie thinks it's a W.O.W.O because he always hears Yucckie scream out OW!, OW! when he takes a shower. In reality, Yucckie screams OW! OW! Because, sometimes when he turns the water back on it's a bit hot or cold. To that, Yucckie always says "no way Mahzie", I like the hot or cold blast because it makes my heart pump and my blood flow flah-zoodily fast! That's Opti-mystically speaking of course.

Water! This great life giving liquid of joy, also created many other "HQ", solutions as it trickled, drained and was creatively re- routed throughout branches and into the arteries of the ultra-natro- recyclo-freindly Morton bay fig tree house perched

91

atop of his most favorite hill & surf viewing spot. Last but not least, to take his mind off of the storm that was on its way, he tucked himself into bed & then played a self made ding dongley song on his hand painted, (*self tuned, to;"My dog has fleas"*) ukulele...ding da ding ding-dong, diggal, lingal da ding ding dong and so on and so on and so on and on.

Yucckie would then say in his mind or aloud, in a warm and comforting voice, "I love you" (*as if someone were there*) and also, "thank you" with focused intentions to the Great Spirit and all of the friends that he would know or knew. Yucckie believed that if good intentions were spoken into the air, it would be like tapping flat water with a stick of joy, and watching the rings of joy & love being sent around the universe. So, that's what Yucckie did without an ego, but as gentle as a landing turtle dove. Eventually he was off to dream seeding land where he could finally let his mind freely go & sleepily rest. Yucckie was aware that when going to sleep with a combination of a happy tune and loving thoughts in his mind, this would open the gates for a river of joy dream seeds that could now easily flow and be seeded into his fertile & musically, mathematically, opti-mystically inclined mind.

That night, Yuckkie quite comfortably snuggled with his hand painted ukulele and allowed the dream seeds to be naturally cultivated in his mind. After all of his careful preparation, Yucckie fell fast asleep in the purest comfort of dreams that were far away from the reality of the tremendous storm that was just beyond the strong squircular walls. Yucckie felt confidently protected in the embraced of the time tested uniquely massive and wondrous "Morten bay fig HQ" tree house, high on top of the hill. Yucckie thought to himself, Thank you Great grand-daddy fig tree, and thank you for sure.

Yuckkie had several different blending dreams scenes that night, but they were, as he would call them "high quality double T dreams". These "high quality double T dreams" (*HQDTD*), were usually of himself and his friends of now, past, and even friends to be. These HQDTD's had them all enjoying amazing clear sunny days. He would either be share-carving high mountain powder on a snowboard with his unique "all-style", riding lines (*that he had learned from some of the best riders & surfers on earth*), surfing perfect exotic twist and spitting tube-ridey-glassy waves, or sessioning the smoothest of concrete & rails at the world's greatest skate parks during the best dry weather days.

Yucckie's dream-time mind would sometimes take him from riding a snowboard with stylishly controlled float-drifting maneuvers across fresh powdery snow covered mountains that then, his board changed to a "Fish style surfboard" and onto a completely new surface to ride. This dream place would then blend into blue, purpley, heavenly hollow ocean-like wave-water tube-rides, which changed but again! This other new change, which was yet another board morph and would turn into a skate-boardie thingy that only a dream mind can trans-blend into things of this sort.

In his dream-seeded mind, Yucckie would then cruise-groove into some sort of a hardened smooth polished surface with all natural curves, handrails and many other things that can only be created in someone's wildest of dream-scaping mind. Each surface, idea or location was of course created beyond utter perfection. Yucckie's dream mind equipment would enable a flow, groovy, jib, slide or grind & always just rightly fit & had the flexibility to explore any surface, size, incline, shape or place that an infinite dreaming imagination could ever want to think of or create!!!! ☺~

In Yuckkie & Mahzie's dreams even, the best of the best great athletes of now, the future, and of before, the ones they called "dream-hood heroes" were part of their core. Amongst them were great surfers, skaters, snowboarders and even people that don't do those things. Their heroes were always tied to a specific moment in time when they were deemed "heroic" by them, and they would always visualize them as such. When Kelly Slater (*in the movie 'Black & White*) had his star trunks moment and became world champion after, so many times more. Danny Way jumping the Great Wall of China was to them, also quite heroic and great. Heroic was Benjamin Franklin, and his story of the lightning striking his kite. Heroic was Thomas Edison and his successful creation of the first bulb of light. Heroic also to them was a man named, Martin Luther King jr. especially while giving the great speech of "The Sermon on the Mount". They were and are always in awe of the many works and discoveries of Steven Hawking and how he gets about. Their heroes include the young, or even the more blessed, and all of their teachers and the standards they upheld. Yucckie and Mahzie praised the heroic efforts of their mums and their dads simply, for looking after them and reading to them joy adventure stories like this one, when they put them to bed.

In their dreams their heroes always acted with "Pure Stoke" passion & sometimes admiration, when they would cheer for anyone. They & their heroes would cheer, not only for the winner but also for someone simply having a go. Yucckie and Mahzie, in their dreams would thank their dream hood as well as all of their heroes, for being there for them. These two were quite grateful for being and having such an amazing dream audience and they felt quite humbled as they put on their dreamtime show. Yucckie & Mahzie's other dream-hood heroes were great peacemakers, philosophers, inventors, poets & even paupers because even a pauper had the ability to be a showstopper.

Some of their heroes were great with animals, like horses or even the birds. Some could ride small boats over massive waterfalls. Some of their heroes were masters of words & board games or climbing up cliff walls. Some of their heroes spent all their time caring for others so they didn't get much time for sports, or glory, or even fame of course. Yucckie & Mahzie wished to share a wave with all of their heroes in a perfect place one day. But for now, in their dreams, they may have to stay. Unless they invent a time machine dream catcher, hmmm, who knows what will become of that thought, one day.

One really important thing that all of their dream-hood heroes had in common (*whether in the dream or out*) was that they were "passionate", without a doubt. This passion that we speak of, for Yucckie, Mahzie or just about anyone, seems to be the core that creates a simple natural flow, with just the right kind of jib or slide-glide, intention, lifestyle or hand-jive. Even a way with words that connects one to a greater source with just the right musical time. This passion & connection to this greater source, was the thing that made the heroic moments such memorable parts of their amazing dreamtime.

The best way to describe Yucckie & Mahzie's infamous styles, or their way of approach, would be "A respectful use of their environment", "Never to encroach". This style or way of living was applied in whatever path, line or medium that they would chose. This "respectful use of their environment" style was utilized, whether surfing, inventing, loving, living, learning, skateboarding, snowboarding or even being just a good friend. Yucckie was once told by one of his heroes, that his, "Simple style of life", may have been a dream of his dreamtime heroes as well. Yucckie thought, "No-wizzipilly-way!!" this would be "quite preposterous", as he thought that his heroes had everything worked out. If they did or did not is another long story to hear maybe from one of them some other day. But to find out more about simple life living ideas, these two are only as far away as your local post office. Send a letter or postcard to Yucckie or Mahzie. The ideas about living a simply life can be requested, only by a hand written letter sent to Yucckie & Mahzie in the post. (Postal *address is found at; www.yucckie.com*)

BUT BACK TO YUCKIES DREAMING – On The following page is a new technology that Yuckkie is currently working on, and is sure to be worked out as time goes on. We have the privilege of being the first to see the Y&M "Open Mind" technology (*otherwise known as "OM Tech"*). This technology when practiced & utilized correctly allows one insights into one's future & one's dreams. Here are some frame grabs of both Yucckie & Mahzie's "OM Tech" dreams seeds, past or future aspirations. Yucckie calls them the "OM tech" Dream seed images. Yucckie and Mahzie believe that if you plant good & honest dream seed images in your fertile minds ground, and cultivate them through your actions, surely the seeds will grow into a forest of joy & success. If this is done and practiced correctly, yourself and many more, you will astound. "Om tech" works, and works well, but like anything, to get good it takes careful practice", and practice you may and you must!

99

This amazing dream illustration is by Stan Squire @ www.stansquire.com

101

Chapter 8- The Great Storm

Just then, smack dab in the middle of Yucckie's most comfortable dream-seeding fast asleep zone, that storm of unbelievable magnitude hit the coastline!! Crash! Bam!! Kaz-rraka-powie!! That storm brought with it winds that swirled, twisted and bent the straight standing trees straight down to the ground, and then bent those same trees over, and right back around! Then it began to rain (*figuratively speaking*) cats, kangaroos and all kinds of other mythical creatures (*disclaimer - in this storm no animals were hurt or treated badly*) from all angles and areas of the sky. With that wild rain came lightning that ignited an inferno of crack-zagally & cold blue-white laser beam flashes, into the space that normally shimmered with a pleasant calm glisten-shimmery moon rise.

Then the thunder pounded like sledge hammers wielded by Thor & the gods of Asgaard, with such immense sounds that the Meer-est of Meer cats and Moli-est of Moles dug 13.34 meters deeper under the ground. Some of the Meer cats & moles dug so deeply that they came out on the other side of the world. On this night, it seemed for a moment that the world turned inside out and upside down. Woah widdely woo ha! Who knows what next would be unfolded on this ever so treacherous of nights, all around?

However, on this wildly torrential eve, because young Yuckkie was so thorough in his preparation, he didn't hear a sound. As the world turned upside down and inside out, his mind was quiet and at peace. Yuckkie slept well and comfortably with a smile on his face throughout the wildly incredible night. Even Yucckie's heart kept an even calm & steady beat (*tap-aka-tap-aka-tap-aka*).

Then as quickly as this storm came, it subsided, with a brand new morning, which arrived as uniquely as it does in most places of beauty. The morning arrived with a lively awakening sunrise, which is never ever boring & always a great sight. The sun gently & steadily climbed high in the sky. The birds and animals came out of their places of safety, chirping and singing a song that couldn't have been orchestrated by anyone other than the creator of all things. This happened with the magical abstract detail of

103

perfectly painted love, patience & care, obviously by a being endowed with infinite kindness.

The flowers that were bent to a kneeling position with petals that had been unfolded & pushed facing down by the great force of the wind & raining sledgehammers, now had changed their downward direction & stood evenly tall. Each flower was uplifted equally by an unearthly levitation that was welcome as they were now free of the invisible stress chains created by the storm. The suns rays lifted each flowering face proudly & high above the muddy soils of the ground without an explanation, or even an audible sound. With the warmth of the sun and the beautiful bird songs, each flower now unbent, found their inner unrelenting strength and reached up to the sky embracing the warming, graceful, engulfing sun's loving rays.

All of these naturally beautiful creatures seemed to now be quite happy to know that the storm had gone. Although its power seemed painful, the storm still left them with the gift of wonderful nourishing clean water to feed & bless them all for many days to come. As with the many amazing natural creatures of the earth, young Yuckkie awoke in a similar way, lifting the sky with his arms, and with a warm smile on his face, humming the same happy tune that he played on his ukulele the night before. Yucckie was now endowed with a mind full of new dream seeds & ready for action, with a new day to see, search and to explore. Every morning without fail both Yuckkie & Mahzie proclaim to themselves "We will greet this day with love in our hearts and we will succeed" at what ever we do, and assist whomever we meet. They did this daily ritual and treated it, as if it were a form of fine art.

With such great daily affirmations, both Yucckie and Mahzie were quite happy most of the time. If ever they felt down, they would always refer to their pocket handbooks or talk to someone, like their dad or their mum. This effort of re-alignment would help to lift up their spirits and put them back on to the mission of learning and the creation of fun. Yuckkie & Mahzie were and are, quite aware of the idea that no matter what one does, we are all somehow connected by an invisible thread which they and I believe is actually made of water. So what one does really may affect everyone and everything. Like tapping a stick on the flat glassy water can send rings from its center to the world of water and even the air around it.

Imagine what would happen, if we were to tap the center of what may be our humanly universally connected water source, with only good intentions of love & of fun of course. This action may just make the world an even more wonderful place. In our minds each one of us can never be just a "one" or an "I" due to our watery connection. Yucckie and Mahzie and I believe, that there really is and always will ever be "We", even if that you, me or I don't believe. This is just the way it is. There truly and gratefully will & must always be simply, "We", never a singular I or a me.

Chapter 9 - A brand new day

This particular after-storm morning, as Yuckkie usually does. Yucckie put on his favorite specially created red silken board shorts, utility belt & comfortable, quite carefully chosen skate shoes. Yucckie then prepared for the day with his own yoga practice, flex bending and stretching, then enjoying a large glass of Mother Nature's finest water imaginable. I would assume that he did this, just as the "Great Spirit" may have intended... while singing a happy song, la di da la diddy doh.

But wait just a minute! (*With great excitement he exclaimed*) He was just near the bottom of his large glass of water, when he quickly remembered the great storm and wondered, what outside has been moved or altered? After such great dreaming and what seemed to be such a glorious morning, he forgot all about the storm and all of the warnings!

What has come of the outside world, he thought? So, he ran to his window to see what had become of the beautiful land, his Morten Bay Fig, "HQ" and beyond. So out of his window, there it was, whew! That was some storm! Look at that, the whole world looks so different, like someone had taken one of those snow globes and shook it up, down and all around! Everything inside, not just the snow got completely rearranged and turned upside down! What?! Widdley wooooo000hiehaho, (*he exclaimed*)! It all looked so out of this worldly now! And what was that massive pile of hooo hah hiddy hup, on the beach which he could see from his hilltop tree house "HQ" without even having to use his binoculars with their HD lenses & 1000x telescopic reach...What the hiddy diddy dip doo dah is that?! Now, there was nothing but silence. For at least this one moment... Yucckie did not, and could not speak.

On the clearing of his beloved surfing beach, which he had walked across so many thousands of times before, were what seemed to look like (*from his hilltop perspective*) thousands, millions, billions and maybe even trillions of little stars! It was quite strange and especially odd you see. It was so strange, that Yucckie didn't even notice the perfection of the offshore wind lifted peaks, long faces and squircular sun kissed tubular barrels

109

that were heaving and spitting (*paatooohf & paahroooohf!!*) up and down his happily shared & most amazing un-crowded secret stretch of beach! Yucckie would have normally been phrophing to be the first in the surf to enjoy all of the tubes in the waves, but not today. Yucckie knew in his mind that there would always be another day to set free his fins and his stylish mucho cool carving personally designed shred lines.

Yucckie screamed out, "oh my biddy bew bizzzmo" that storm musta been so mega-massive that it must have rrrRIPPED the stars right out of the sky and crash landed them rrrright onto the beach! Yucckie thought to himself, I'd better get down there quick smart and see if I can help those little stars get back into the sky or who knows what will happen to our beloved universe, & what else may be unleashed! This was really quite worrisome to Yucckie, because of his passion for the stars & the heavens above, now he also thought what would become of the night sky? With no points of light or even spaces in between, just emptiness and loneliness for as far as the eye could infinitely see!

Yucckie always thought that there was an interesting irony with regard to storms, for both surfers and those that ride or rode the mountains of snow. This irony was that each of the massive storms that have created such bliss for snow riders and surfers might have left a path of destruction in their aftermath somewhere else. What an interesting quandary in his mind this created. This is most likely why he was always so intent on helping those in need of assistance, and why he also create harmless but helpful solutions for all.

"No! I won't be a Beatle & just let it be (*Yucckie exclaimed*). "I will do whatever it may take, or whatever it may need" are the words that came to mind for Yucckie. These words came to mind with a mirror of the same thought, I'm quite sure, from his good friend in Mahzie who lives on the other-side of town. Great minds think alike some say. Well, it is for sure that great minds did think a like, on this particular day. I may need a bit of help he thought, as even the famous Rock & Roll, "The Beatles" needed a little help from their friends.

Chapter 10 - A Friend in Need is a Friend Indeed

With a touch of a button, and the "phhuuum" cool laptop starting up sound, he powered up on his laptop, downloaded and set up his communication software of choice and contacted all of his friendly friends that were around. Yucckie even called all of his not so friendly friends that he could see were logged on. He loved his friend's all just the same, friendly or not, he asked them all to come out to help on this day as they may even be in need of bull dozer or a crane.

Yucckie then blasted out messages on all of his social networking pages hoping to get a massive response. He called his best & most trusted friend Mahzie to help with the cause. He then contacted "J.C." at the radio station, and Travs (*the smartest friend that he ever had ever known*). Travs was interesting in that he never had to use his ears. Strange as it may sound, he always wore headphones under his thicker than thick beanie. So, created did Travs, an invention what he called voice to txt sunglasses (*VTS*). This special invention of his, would instantly write all words as they were spoken, by anyone around him on his sunglass lenses. All he had to do was read his lenses to know what was going on. To this I said, Oh Wow! This creative creation would allow him to just read the words rather than ever having to hear a sound? Imagine how many problems could be solved once word of this clever invention one gets out.

Then there was Flat cat (*the "Cat of instant Karmic reaction"*) to help hopefully without (*no pun intended*) a pause. If that Flat Cat, didn't believe in a lightning strike, he would be sure to be struck by lightning, with in a matter of seconds of his comments against such a possibility or such an unheard of event coming within any close proximity of his mouth which was usually full of lazy days long lasting yarns. He was a bit of a silly cat, that cat of Flat. His flatness was due to his humor and also his physical thinness, which made his profile a vertical line. When he turned sideways and showed you his profile, all you could really see were his feet, nose, hat, and a part of a smile.

Yucckie left a message for another friend named Wingo (*the non-flying very pessimistic bluebird that lived in the bird cage under one of the root branches of Grand daddy Fig tree*"). Then he called his not so friendly friends including, Arro & Gance (*who were never good when they got together, just imagine that*). He also

113

called the pack of wild and "good only for wool" sheep that followed Arro & Gance around (*they were known as the scatter gang, none of whom for some reason or another ever hung around with Yuckkie very much unless it was to get a free lunch*). No matter, Yucckie loved them all just the same, and needed all of them to assist, especially today of all days.

I think that Yucckie & Mahzie both found it hard to hang out with the scatter-gang. Whenever they started up or rode their extra loud "look-at-me" motor-bikes, that were oh so ridiculously loud, that every time they turned the throttle they would wake up all of the babies & people sleeping in and around town. These babies would then cry and would scream, making their mums and dads so sad, and this gang of scatter, they would just say, too bad so sad! It always seemed, that the Scatter Gang when lead by Arro & Gance were a bit selfish & unkind. Just imagine that!

In the long run of life, anyone acting with selfish unkindness on our planet, where we all share the same air, food, water and space, will of course just eventually be let down...hmmm with a "too bad and so sad" which would be the words that they themselves may have to Karmic-ly face one day. The scatter gang and Arro & Gance may have shown up that day, because they were so grateful for the surround-sound-specialized adjustable-

114

headphone-helmets (*SSSAHH*) that Yucckie & Mahzie had made for them. These highly inventive helmets made the "Outside Loud Noise" or (*OLN*) completely go away. The super disturbing OLN would now be only heard by those that wore them. Bravo! What a great invention!

This incredibly thoughtful "OLN" solving invention, funneled the sound back into the helmets, so that those that wore them could enjoy the loud noise, that was loved so much by them. It even took into account some great advice from Yucckie & Mahzie's old friend, Peanut butta who said, "Some people believe that the noise that the Look- at-me cycles makes, is a way to keep look-at-me-motor-cyclists safe on busy roads". So, with that tid bit of great information and IATA in mind, Yucckie & Mahzie installed what they called a "ventro-quick-casting-sensor-module"(*VQCSM*) that could quite quickly cast or throw the noise in any direction, if and when urgently needed.

Yes, with this "VQCSM" module (*just like a ventriloquist throws their voice*) could cause the look-at-me-cycle rider wearing a "SSSAHH" helmet, to direct all of its noise to the ears of a driver of a potentially dangerous vehicle when in traffic, in an effort to be heard & to keep those "look-at-me-motor-bike" riders safer on the roads. This invention, will of course allow all mums, dads and

115

babies and even you & I to sleep well through the night. Sleeping comfortably and dreaming is very important. I hope you agree, as well because, Yucckie and Mahzie believe that sleeping and dreaming may even be our universal right!

Yucckie and Mahzie even cared & care for their not so friendly friends. This great new invention would then be sure to not wake sleeping babies or even shatter the quintessential silence of any happily quaint and quiet sleepy neighborhood. In this case both Yucckie & Mahzie relied on that old saying coming into effect that "A friend in need is a friend indeed ". They knew that they could never have too many friends and would rather have nobody, which they could ever know as an enemy.

So, it is with great joy, I must note on this special day, that they all said the same thing quite amazingly to them. "We will be there to help you for sure, and absolutely to be a part of the solution or the cure." Wow! Because of the care & the fact that Yuckkie & Mahzie chose to be friends with all, even the not so friendly friends (*both big & both small*) everyone still treated these two so respectfully well. This fact helped Yucckie & Mahzie to know that most of their friends would be there for them when they needed a great solution or teamwork to really come together and make everything really gel.

116

So this is how the day went, after calling, emailing, texting, Skype-ing, Viber-ing, Facebook-ing, Zofar-ing, Twitter-ing, Face-timing, Snap-Chatting, Linkedin-ing, I-messaging, You-ku-ing, Weibo-ing, You-tubing, We-chatting, Pinteresting, Drum-messaging, smoke-signaling, Instagram-ing, carrier-pigeoning, Google plus-ing & even "bottle messaging" (*the later because he heard it in song by a great master musician called Sting*) all his friends & not so friendly friends, due to the situation he skipped his morning ("*W.O.W.O*") which was o.k. because, he had one the night before, oh yea! Yucckie threw on some clothes, made and ate an incredibly healthy super food breakfast, grabbed his skateboard with the natural sort of super styley grace like that of a majestic mother eagle skimming the surface of the forest to pick up twigs to create a nest for its eggs, and headed out of the door.

Skateboarding with Yucckie & Mahzie was amazing because they would never pass a piece of trash or rubbish on the road, curb or grass. They both would take the mess quite personally & would make it a point to scoop it up with out stopping, while basket-ball-tossing it in a city trash bin, scoring mental points on their mindful charts with laughs, new carves and a shredful slash as they got it in to the bin made for the trash!

This day, Yuckkie & Mahzie surf-skateboarded their way all the way down to the beach. The beach was Yucckie & Mahzie's natural place of comfort and was always filled for some reason with the wonderful warm coco buttery smells of summer, no matter what time of year that it was. Now, when I say surf skateboarded, I really mean it! Yuckkie read the road, curbs, sidewalks handrails & all of its curves & surfaces and even saw the trees as if they were the heaving ocean waves or majestic snow carvable mountains, with an eye to ride them in a similar surf fashion. With super styley mastery & graceful perfection, Yucckie could carve across the concrete & across the grass spraying imaginary crescent shaped fans of water blasting high up in the air, splashing out like peacock feathers in their glorious full show. While no one, gardener, carpenter, mom, judge or businessman seemed to care or to know. If they did care or take notice Yucckie and Mahzie would invite them along for sure!

Yuckkie found the most unique & amazing ways to tuck up into a higher line, up under tree branches that were overgrown & bending over sidewalks as if he was getting one of those mystical 20 second tube rides that most surfers dream to share. Yucckie always remembered good intentions, with his respectful & peace-giving way, before he untraceably slashed the grass or tube rode through the trees as always. Yucckie thought to himself and even sometimes said aloud, respectfully; "thank you with honor, for your shared time oh, trees, grass & clouds". To Mahzie and others he'd say "I love you brother or sister", and I couldn't have shared this great day without you" which in his mind, is one way to make a happier, you, I, me or we! It takes a lot of good you, I & me's to make an action-filled great group, of the best kind of we's!

With their special skateboard adventure vision, they even found vertical walls to ride up and fly across gaps filled with stairs while doing quad-droople Mctwists or Terje Haakonsen flips, & Shaun White, Rune Glifberg, Flynn Novak, Clay Marzo, Dane Reynolds maneuvers with all the right kinds of grabs, twists & spins. On these days, there was never a panel of imaginary judges. For judgment, neither Yucckie nor Mahzie seemed to care. Yucckie & Mahzie's styles were said by some to truly have been hotter than any hot sauce that has ever been made, but still cooler than ice cream on the hottest summer days.

Yucckie & Mahzie's style of riding reflected the kind of fun that is always better when shared by more than just one. While shredding or carving quite joyfully Yucckie & Mahzie would sometime notice another "friend to be", sitting alone on a front step, verandah or porch along the way. These two with their friendliness ways, would always ask that person to join them for some simple exercise and fun to be had for someone, who may have otherwise had another lonely lazy day, laid out in front of them. They liked to include anyone in the fun things that life may have to offer, with never a thought that would or may offend.

Yucckie & Mahzie seemed to always make new friends in a collective sort of way. Keeping in touch was paramount and they would do it as often as needed, as this was never a problem for them. A post card, an email or even better a visit throughout the passing days was always up to them, and so, just that they did as often as they may.

Just as they got to the end of the road where the asphalt and the beach make friends, Mahzie slid off of a curb where their hands instantly locked into a misty hi-fiving-slap-wiggle-secret-hand shake with Yucckie that is only known of between them. Of course, Yucckie & Mahzie will be happy to show you this hi-fiving-slap- wiggle-secret-hand shake, when ever you get to meet them.

Well, Yucckie & Mahzie did all of this amazing stuff, having fun the whole way while making their way down to the beach. Down at the beach they found that it wasn't the stars from the sky at all. It was even worse. It was actually all of the starfish from the bottom of their beloved sea that had washed up on the beach! Both the young & even the most blessed starfish had been dragged up on to the hotter than really hot sauce, and ever so dangerous hot sandy shore. Now Yucckie thought, we are in "Reeeeeeeeeaaal Tribibity trouble" because the sun this morning was getting Reeeeeeeeealllly hibibidy Hot! The weather report said that the air temperature would be hotter then freshly-cooked-pizza-cheese that could even burn the roof or your mouth, for the rest of the week! Which meant, these poor non-walking starfish would all surely dry up and perish in the suns summer heat! If these little starfish all perish in one big Giffify Gafaah! So many more issues could unfold or unravel due to our watery connected connection. To this Yucckie exclaimed, oh no & lah di dah di dah what to do!?

Yucckie & Mahzie thought again, being that we are all water-connected to one another somehow, in some magical and maybe even scientific way, to even the starfishes in all of the world's great ocean-og-raphies. What could or would this do to our underwater bio-system or how would this effect the lands of the world, without this special part of this sea of "We" inter-connectivity? A long and drawn out disaster for sure is possible, and most likely. This may even kick off a new evolution of starfish

121

causing them t walk upright & hand in hand with you and me!

Yucckie & Mahzie in their solutions & solving sort of way, thought to themselves "We are gonnafix-it"? We are gonnafix-it and fix it we must today! It's gonna take more than the two that is you and me, for this particular situation, it's really gonna take, what they call, a whole lot of we's! As with solving most of the world's issues it is really about finding ways for all of the we's to agree. Yucckie & Mahzie know that by using the great power of, "love & kindness" all we's can solve all and any issues, most completely, peacefully & most sus-tain-ably.

Chapter 11 – Success With Persistence

Now, Yuckkie & Mahzie in their different but pioneering ways were usually the first to find the truth of most situations and were also the first characters down on the beach that amazing morning. They decided to do the most responsible thing and get to work right away! Yucckie & Mahzie were also quite sure that all of their friends & not so friendly friends, once they saw what they saw and got the call, from where ever they were, would be there quite quickly, and quickly for sure! Yuckkie & Mahzie decided to focus their wildly creative minds, and right there and then decided that they would together begin. They, if only a dynamic duo, were going to somehow save all of the starfish, and try not to leave one behind.

So Yuckkie & Mahzie got to work right away and when all of their friends & not-so-friendly friends arrived they got them into the huddles of all huddles to create a master plan. With a special strength, loyalty, & honest conviction and lots of IATA in mind they got to work all together with all of the true friends that they could find. All that were there did as they did. There was only one that wasn't there, right away, one who had yet to decide, what to do on this day. This did not matter because the ones that were there all knew what to do. No matter how hard it would or may be, today it was up to them to save all of the starfish and get them back to the sea. Yucckie, Mahzie and all of this crew, knew that the sun was only getting hotter and higher in the sky and if they didn't move fast, surely they would all perish & some could even fry! Oh my, my, my!

All of them and even some more made it down to the beach to help out that day, to share & care in all kinds of amazing great ways. Yucckie & Mahzie even thought that they saw some of their dream-hood heroes there. With all that had to be done it was hard to know if their dream hood heroes were there for sure. But heroes they all became on that amazing day. So many kind folks and not-so-kind-folks came out to assist. Unbelievably even Arrow, Gance, and the rest of the scatter gang, who were usually a bit too busy doubling for couch cushions or making their "look-at-me cycles" louder & more look-at-me-able were there showing an interesting new found sort of care.

It was strange to see them helping, but it was great to see them nonetheless in this time that could have been not so nice and full of un-needed extra stress. Yuckkie & Mahzie aren't & weren't two, that could or can leave anyone out of any new adventure or anything difficult or fun for that matter. Yuckkie & Mahzie always tried to have an all-inclusive plan. The story of how Yucckie & Mahzie met Arrow, Gance and the Scatter gang, is of course another long lions tale that we will tell you about one day soon, when you read the next book in this series of a few.

And it was, one by one and sometimes two by two & three & then four and five that Yucckie, Mahzie and all that came to assist, gently picked each starfish up and gave them joyful giggly smiles, while getting them safely off the highly heated & sizzling hot, sandy sea shore. To each starfish, kind words were then spoken. These kind words were said to be; "we love you little starfish's go back and be free"! Each friend noticed, the starfish seemingly smiling back as to say" thank you" just before each was spin-skipped back into their wonderful, and now quite calm, shining, deep purple, blue-green, dreamy sea-world. It has been said that, one, two or maybe even three-hundred of the starfish may have possibly been heard to yell out what sounded like a massive Wow wow & Whoooo-pie weee! as they whizzed across their not so high

125

position in the sky, back into their cool watery world to get back to their joyful lives in the sea.

Fun was always with Yuckkie & Mahzie, so work it was not, and they and their friends merrily tossed, skipped and spun each starfish one by one without problem (*even though some would have complained, "its terribly hot"*). Yucckie & Mahzie inherently shared the same motto of; "The difficult we do immediately & the impossible simply, is not". They never complained, they just got and get on with whatever needs to be done...& done it will be. With them most things are done with fun, even when for some.fun.it is not.

Hours and hours went by and it had seemed that they had tossed, skipped and spun many more than one and at least a thousand & some back into the sea. But, when they looked back onto the beach, it seemed like only a few had been saved. Still, they worked on and on and on and gave their time just to save another's life. After a few more hours of day, their old friend Wingo (*the non-flying pessimistic bluebird that chose to live in an open bird cage and also chooses not to fly, but says he could if he wanted to, but always puts flying off for maybe some other time! We don't know why for sure, we think he has simply always been too afraid to try*) arrived at the beach. Wingo's situation is an unfortunate one, as he was born with such beautiful wings and an aerodynamic form that was obviously created to glide freely across the incredible expanse of the breathtaking skies. Yucckie wondered why he hadn't been born with wings. He always imagined that if he had wings, all he would do all day, would be to explore the wind waves of the sky. One day I'm sure he will figure out an answer to his question of why, or possibly create his own winged contraption that will take him high, or even higher than the sky.

Wingo who lives just next to Yuckkie's "HQ" high up on the hill top", had finally wandered down to the beach to speak to young Yuckkie and his friends. As per usual, Wingo who is always quite worried about what might happen if he gives something different a go, but always talks himself and many others around him out of even thinking of trying anything new, brought his pessimistic ways with him today. Yucckie and Mahzie were ready with the right answer for Wingo, you might say. Wingo said to young Yuckkie, who was now halfway through, doing his best at saving a trillion or more starfish from losing their lively zest. "Yuckkie", "I've been watching you and your silly friends all morning since before my usual waking hour of ten am". I've been watching you wild characters run around in squircles to no end. I've been watching you all run back and forth, skipping these

127

starfish back into the sea and I have to ask you this question. What do you think that you are doing & for what will it be? There are way too many starfish here on the beach to make a difference. Why don't you just forget about it and go back to bed and let them all perish. It's the natural way, so you may as well, just let them go today."

Yuckkie & Mahzie (*the boys who love everything & everyone*) stopped to think about this uncommon question for exactly 13:34 minutes & seconds in perfect unison. This 13:34 minutes & seconds was a strange & odd measure of time to recall. This measure of time seemed to be a lifetime as far as minutes & seconds go, for all that waited, as though they were put on hold. It was like being put in a holding pattern on a phone call, by a customer service robot message on a never-ending telephone company call. For many, patience was truly being tested once again.

Each minute & second seemed more like hours. This was like time as it does, had simply slowed down. Was it in our imagination or was this snails pace of 13:34 minutes & seconds a reality show in the making? I'm not sure if anyone ever really knows how or why time speeds up and slows down, but it did slow down just then for sure! For the first time ever Yuckkie & Mahzie seemed for only those moments to be in utter perplexion, in their minds about that strange question. Hmmmmmm was the first sound to come from the now pursed lips of their otherwise infinitely smiling mouths.

They both thought & said simultaneously in multiple "hmmmmmmm's, being that they were thinking for the greater "We", not just an "I", "she", or a, "he". Thankfully for sure they remembered just then something that they had read in one of those dusty old books that Yucckie's father & mother had given to them!!!! ☺ One phrase that read, "As long as you persist, surely you will succeed" and the other that was their life philosophy was; to, "Love one another as I have loved you that ye also love one another" which is said to be quoted from the heavens above, in a book by a man called John. With these simple ideals, is how they did their best to live, think, dream and believe.

On this day, Yuckkie & Mahzie's overwhelming compassion for all life became quite evident by their actions. Like a synchronized flash of lightning and a synchronized thunder blast of exhilarating but somehow peacefully light loving laughter, both Yuckkie & Mahzie hooted as they looked on the ground beneath their feet. Each of them picked up the starfishies, those were helplessly lying there beside their big feet, and finally said to

129

Wingo; "Why don't you and we get together as three & gently toss these helpless little star-fishes back into the sea", Hmmm you might say, what an interesting team of three.

Now with this new lead team of three, you will see how much of a difference was made for the job of setting these little star-fishies free. Never before did Wingo lend a hand, but with this sort of synchro-support assisting him to stand, and on this interesting day, which was quite odd for most and all, one might say Wingo thought, ok. I'll give it a try. This time I can't really get hurt & those helpless starfish are so cute and small, yes we must together, save them all. So, happily together they spun & skipped them back into the sea.... Then with a synchronized giggle and a glint, the sun sparkled in their eyes, but didn't make them squint. Yuckkie & Mahzie smiled proudly because they knew that they had found another helper to help beyond his own quest, just like in an old poem at the Minjunbal cultural center about "the saving of the starfish" that they had read a long time before this moment, which has now come true at best.

The un-expectable happened just then. Without even considering anything more, some unknown magical timing caused that pessimistic, non-flying bluebird to lift up his wings, maybe just to stretch or even to shake some dust off, but never to fly or soar.

"Strangely Bizarre" is the most creative Wiki-splanation that "I" or the Internet could ever muster about the splendid profundity of this particular moment. Yes, I say, as luck would have it, at that same moment a soft breeze began to breeze and naturally by the shape of Wingo's wings, part of Bernoulli's great aero-dynamical theory came into being. That wonderfully needed soft but strong breeze, with just the right angle and gusting that lifted that un-flying bluebird right up off of his stiffly bent knees!

Like a beautifully redeemed angel, Wingo was lifted high up above even that of the greatest and most majestic tall forest trees. Of course just then Wingo's natural, but hidden flying bird instincts set in. Wingo began to flap his wings as he pleased. He seemed to "Lift the sky & push the ground" but wow, it all happened so fast and came to him with such ease. This was Wingo's absolute moment of "Euphoria" as he had just entered his "unknown zone". Wow, what an amazing moment to share. Everyone that was there on the beach that day watched in amazement and at the glory of this great change in their friend Wingo as he soared across the air. Wingo had now, in a Bob Marley-ian philosophication, been "Emancipated from his own mental slavery" and was so gracefully, magically & euphorically set free.

"Awareness of our wings", is when each and every one of us becomes truly able to soar to great heights and also has the ability to help others to experience life's great gifted journeys and other amazing things. In this case Wingo the now high-flying bluebird decided to sing a grateful & what seemed to be a song of his own liberation that could be heard from all across the land & sea. His song came with words of his own that I am quite sure, was meant to be sung, around the world by many a "We" including the "we" that is you and is me.

Wingo's song went something like this... with a whistling introduction, maestro won't you please....*whew, whew whew whi whhew, whi whew,whi whew, whi,whi, whhoooh, whhi, whhi, whhii whhi,whew,whi,whew,whi,whi,whew whooh.."* Happy to be here, *happy to be here, ...We can laugh and sing or fly all day, we can sing a song any old way now, we're gonna do it our own way, happy to be...ta daa da da, ta di da di daa daa, gonna do it our own way happy to be. We can think, & live, or just smile all day, or we can sing a song any old way now, we're gonna do it our own way, Happy to be....etc, etc, etc.*

All the friends & even the ones that were not so-friendly friends joined in and sang for the rest of the afternoon while they went on saving the starfish, until they had finally saved them all.

132

Yuckkie and his friends decided to "be the change" on that propitious day and they hope that you will do the same in your own punctilious and wonderful way.

Oh my good giddy gaahsismo! Somehow with all the excitement, we forgot to mention what occurred on the very next day. Yuckkie woke up in his classically Yuckkie way. He surf skateboarded all the way down to that same beach in his same magically amazing and wonderful way. But something new caught his attention. Yucckie noticed a smallish sea beaten & battered treasure chest with a worn out, wet and salty bit of paper attached to it, with starfish handwriting on it, which read.

"Thank you, to Yuckkie & Mahzie and all of your friends for saving us. This is just an old chest that we found at the bottom of the sea which we would like to give to you, as a gift for saving our lives!"

Yucckie opened this interesting small box and this is what he found after twisting open its lock. Inside this salted, smallish, worn-by-the sea box was a largish skeleton key wrapped up quite tightly in some silken red fabric that seemed quite familiar, kind of like that special fabric of Yucckie's, which could be, and is quite likely. Around this key was another handwritten letter. The letter said this and not very much more;

"It has been said that this key unlocks a box that holds a small sack of what may be the last remaining seeds of the great Care- lock trees. Of this magnificent and massive great breed of trees there were seven. One on each continent with an unground root system that spanned the entire earth, and this connection actually almost did happen a long time ago. Once planted the underground root system will with time become inter-connected to create a global underground magical web of love, peace, caring & prosperity that would forever protect the earth & all of humanity for eternity. These

glorious trees had a similar look to that of Great Grand daddy fig tree, except 30 times the size. In the beginning of time these great trees were here on our great green & blue marble of a planet but, mankind came along as it does & may do, and just before the last one connected about one year or two, they chopped them & shredded them down to create lovely doors, tables, chairs, toothpicks and other things that seemed to be needed, even small chairs for dolls to be seated."

Hmmmmmmmm? This was very interesting information, to say the least.

The letter then stated that, *the receiver of this note is needed to heed it. If you please, these great Care-lock trees must be replanted & maintained in each of the continents by two close friends, with a triangular 3rd that is of your blood alike, who will be the key, only for reasons that you will then come to see. There is none to blame or to be ashamed, for not knowing what things may have been. Now that we are aware, we should do, our best to protect & reconnect this great forest at least for the successful futures of the we that is the you and the me! Aware of what we use, aware of what we do, awareness is one of the great keys of a successful life, but really has only been remembered by just the lucky few!*

This letter was signed, *the "We" that was a you, I or me?*

Yucckie & Mahzie's destiny has now been set with a great task. As our new close friend, please join us because together we can really make good & great changes that will truly happen and sustainably become love, infinitely.

"Wow woozoodily whoopee!! Yuckkie exclaimed!! Another great adventure! Time to get ready! We can get on a traveling skateboard, bike, boat or even on an airplane. Not just a new adventure, but a chance to make new friends, to be kind & to love all and beyond. "The things that may happen along the many journeys, will allow us to create solutions for a better and greater good change".

And so it happened, and happens everyday that the world loves Yucckie and Mahzie and all those that choose to be and to live as they. You will find out much more when you read the next books in this series about different ways to be, think, give and even live.

It has been through the hunger for the mastery of learning, healthy living, kindness to all, surfing, skateboarding & snowboarding that our friends have learned to honor & manage life's great transitions. We have learned to improvise, adapt & quite humbly overcome life's many environments of change. Please share with us your story about what & how you have done the same. Email Yucckie & Mahzie at;

Yucckie@yucckie.com or Mahzie@yucckie.com

Remember always, that you are truly AMAZING!

"Golden Envelope in the back of the book"

Contact Yucckie & Mahzie by email to receive your personalized golden envelope today!

Yucckie@yucckie.com or Mahzie@yucckie.com

Philosophized Glossarized Yuccki-phied Definitions

Affinity-*A passionate thought about a lifestyle, thing or way of being.*

Antiquities- *An item or thing, from a specified historical period during the ancient past.*

Apps – *An abbreviation for applications. App means application in for a computer, smart phone, tablet or I-pad.*

Arro + Gance = *arrogance – overbearing + pride evidenced by a superior manner toward those whom are thought to be inferiors. To Yucckie there are no inferiors; love is the great equalizer of all mankind, animal kind, and plant kind. Love is universal; let love be the answer to your questions. Be love*

Asgaard - *The heavenly residence of the Norse gods and slain heroes of war.*

Auspicious- *Conducive to success; favorable: "an auspicious moment to hold an election"*

Bananasaurus – *An eco-friendly, automatic air fresher system for cars in warm climates, invented by Yucckie.*

The Beatles- *The Beatles were an English rock band formed in Liverpool in 1960. They became the most commercially successful*

142

and critically acclaimed act in the history of popular music.

Benjamin Franklin-*April 17, 1790) was one of the Founding Fathers of the United States. A noted polymath, Franklin was a leading author, printer, political theorist, politician, postmaster, scientist, musician, inventor, satirist, civic activist, statesman, and diplomat.*

Bernoulli's principle of flight- *the air above a wing tends to move faster than the air below it. According to Bernoulli's Principle, slower air has higher pressure than faster air. That means that the air pressure pushing up on the bottom of the wing is greater than the pressure pushing down, so the wing goes up.*

Be the Change- *"Be the change" - by, Mahatma Gandhi*

Blissful - *Extremely happy; full of joy. Providing perfect happiness or great joy*

Bob Marley- *(6 February 1945 – 11 May 1981), more widely and commonly known as Bob Marley, was a Jamaican singer-songwriter and musician.*

Bodyboard(ing) – *a style of surfing while lying down on a soft board that can give one a different perspective than stand up surfing or knee boarding. Lots of fun!*

Bodysurfing- *riding waves without a board, only the use of ones body. Lots of fun!*

143

Boss- *something really good- (that is a really boss idea, dude!)*

Bottle messaging- *writing a message on a piece of paper then rolling it up and sending off in a river, or any body of water to carry it to anyone that will pick it up, an unknown receiver*

Bottom turn – *this is the most important turn when surfing a wave. This turn decides your direction as well as being the deciding factor and set up for the rest of the ride, which may turn out to be the ride or the wipeout of your lifetime*

Calm – *Being calm is the best way to be, relax a bit and take your time when doing things. "Haste makes waste", when you are not calm many mistakes can be made. Calm is king.*

Caring- *The ability to feel responsible for matters outside oneself. For example – I care about you and I care about the future of our world.*

Care-lock tree- *7 Mythical interconnected universe trees, that when planted in the 7 continents of the earth and allowed to grow to full fruition, will create a special force field protecting the powers of love peace and prosperity on earth and in the universe infinitely.*

Carrier pigeon- *Usually a pigeon or trained bird that was used to carry messages that were tied to its leg to far away lands and would return with an answer.*

Carved (carving)- *an artistic work or path taken when, surfing, snowboarding or skateboarding, etc. in an always connected & cursive sort of way etc.*

Cherokee- *A member of the native North American people of the southeastern US, now mostly living in Oklahoma and North Carolina, but some all over the world. The language of this people has had its own script since 1820.*

Chief Joseph-*The Native American Chief Joseph headed the Wallowa ... while also avoiding violence at all costs, becoming a legendary peacemaker.*

Cinematragic-televivonic-drama-matic– *extremely over dramatic stories shown in the cinema or on television. Yucckie feels that life has so much natural drama, that he chooses not to inundate himself with more. Both Yucckie and Mahzie wish only to surround themselves with kindness. Yucckie and Mahzie also do their best to create love, kindness, and good-clean- fun for all!*

Close-out – *In surfing when a wave forms like a wall across the ocean and falls over itself all at the same time, in one big explosion of water. These waves are generally not ridden, but watched in awe due to the power unleashed all in one big explosive gafaah!*

Compass- *An instrument containing a magnetized pointer that shows the direction of magnetic north and bearings from it.*

Compassion-*is the virtue of empathy for the suffering of others. It is regarded as a fundamental part of human love, and a cornerstone of greater social interconnection and humanism – foundational to the highest principles in philosophy, society, and personhood. Displaying kindness and concern for others. The work or practice of looking after those unable to care for themselves, esp. the sick and the elderly.*

145

Confident- *Feeling or showing certainty about something.*

Cool- *Cool is an aesthetic of attitude, behavior, comportment, appearance and style, although Yucckie believes that nobody is truly cool unless they truly care about the well being of others and take action to ensure that everyone is cared about and cared for.*

Coolsmart - *a person that cares and is compassionate for all, no matter who or how they may be.*

Cooking – *Cooking is preparing food for yourself or someone else to consume. (Always do this with love, care & joy in mind, because the truth is "you are what you eat")*

D.E.W.K *(w duchess)* – *diamond eyed wisdom keeper or grannie & grand pops Definitions- the most mutually agreed upon explanation of a word.*

Dream hood- *Yucckie's dream neighborhood, a special place in ones mind that only you are aware of.*

Dream hood heroes - *People that are passionate about the creation of peaceful solutions, philosophies, music, & inventions. Yucckie's list includes without an end; His Papa, his Mum, Martin Luther King jr., Jesus Christ, Buddha, The Dalai lama, Bhaskaracharya, Sojourner Truth, Benjamin Franklin, Dr. Suess, Mahatma Gandhi, Mother Theresa, Sister Lourdes, Nichidatsu Fujii, Galeleo, The Eco Warrior, Mark Twain, Khan Abdul Ghaffer*

146

Khan, Our friend Philbert, The Wright Brothers, Jacque Cousteau, Socrates, Leonardo Da Vinci, Chief Joseph, Pocohantas, Sequoia, Helen Caldicott, "John Henry the steel driving man", The lifted Lorax. and so many more as there are and will be for sure!

Dream seeds-*knowledge and thoughts that come from a universal source that are show up in all kinds of ways for each of us when we become open true to listening and learning.*

Drum messaging- *Sending messages by drum beats to anyone within hearing distance.*

Edutainment- *a combination of education and entertainment. Both Yucckie and Mahzie believe that education is and creates new pathways to fun, enlightenment and greater experiences. Edutainment is a key to joy while becoming educated.*

Emancipation-*e·man·ci·pate- e·man·ci·pat·ed, e·man·ci·pat·ing, e·man·ci·pates. 1. To free from bondage, oppression, or restraint; liberate.*

Exhilaration- *The act of enlivening or a gladdening.*

Fertile- *(of soil) Producing or capable of producing abundant vegetation or crops, (of a seed or egg) Capable of becoming a new individual.*

Fish-vantage – *Yucckie believes that there are secret advantages*

147

of surfing on a fish shaped surfboard – therefore he defines them as fish-vantages. A fish seems to paddle or plane better on the water. If you have the right fish surfboard it works well in 1 to 8 ft+ if you are surf-fit of course. A proper fish will fit in the boot or trunk of most cars, can be carried on the bus, can fit under your bed, and even looks good hanging on your wall over head.

Foundation- *The lowest load-bearing part of a building, typically below ground level.*

Float drifting- *a style of carving or riding a mountain, an ocean wave, the airwaves or the wonderful world of smooth hardened surfaces.*

Friendly friends- *People with whom you have great & meaningful magnetic relationships with and for some reason click with.*

Future- *the future is definite. It is what you do now that will create your future.*

Gafaah- *final release, exhalation, or sigh of breath*

Gazooosh!- *The sound a of massive surf barrels when they spit one out of a really big tube ride, sound an avalanche makes when it releases it energy from a looming cornice.*

Golden Era- *The good days past, filled with many blessings for all*

Gooby-gew- *something not so nice, slimey, poohey or smelly.*

Google- *Google Search (or Google Web Search) is a web search engine owned by Google Inc. Google Search is the most-used search engine on the World Wide Web, receiving several hundred million queries each day through its various services.*

GPS – *Global Positioning Satellite*

Handshake- *an act of shaking a person's hand with one's own, there are many styles, but always shared as greeting, a goodbye or and act or brotherhood, sisterhood, etc.*

Hand writing (*cursive or script*) - *Writing with a pen or pencil, having the successive letters stylistically joined together.*

Helen Caldicott- *Founded the Women's Action for Nuclear Disarmament (WAND) in the United States, which was later renamed Women's Action for New Directions. It is a group dedicated to reducing or redirecting government spending away from nuclear energy use towards what the group perceives as unmet social issues.*

Heavy – *(ie:that's heavy dude) bad news or hard news from or about somebody.*

High-Falootan- *High falootan!- of high attitude*

High quality dreams- *good time dreams that are so good that the dreams themselves are bound to happen or be created one day. So good that you remember all the details and you have to tell your friends about them. In these dreams also spending time with one or all of ones dream-hood heroes.*

Hollyweird - *There is a place in California that has been known by many to produce entertainment for many people of the world. Having traveled to this place, Yucckie and Mahzie believe that Hollywood and many of the morals and the ideas that are created there are not relevant to their life styles, so they do their best to avoid the ones that are dangerous to their joy. This is why they have named this place Hollyweird, not to put it down as to them weird is simply strange and something that they are unsure of.*

Hotter than hot sauce (HTHS)- *something of high temperature, exceptionally pleasing to the eye, good to look at, or even just a great experience.*

H Q -*Headquarters*

Hug -*An act of holding someone tightly in one's arms, typically to express mutual affection, to embrace someone lovingly.*

Hula-hoop theory of Personal space- *Yucckie found that around the world every culture has a different sense of personal space, so his theory is that all people should be given a hula hoop to exercise with and to also have there personal space kept in tact. Each person no matter how big or small should be allowed at minimum this amount of space when, talking, playing or just enjoying a stroll through the park.*

Intelligence- *The ability to acquire and apply knowledge and skills*

Instagram- *an online photo-sharing & social networking service* that enables its users to take a picture, apply a digital filter to it, and share it on a variety of social networking services, including its own and other leading sites such as Facebook or Twitter

Kaswizzeling- *an interesting new spring-zingy sound from the springs of new invention.*

Kickcccccccccccrrrrrrrrrk!- *sound your skateboard makes when grinding a curb or on some handrails.*

Kite-boarding- *riding a board on the water or snow while being towed by a wind driven kite. Great fun!*

KM's – *short for kilometers. a metric measurement for long distances.*

Laptop-shell-cladded-squircular-tree-pod homes – *specialty tree & on-or-in-ground houses/homes built with only recycled materials, and cladded with old lap-top, mobile, phone and computer shells. These homes were invented by Yucckie & Mahzie out of pure necessity and accessibility of materials.*

Legacy- *An amount of money or property left to someone in a will.*

Liberation- *to be; or to set (someone) free from enslavement or imprisonment.*

Line-up – *a place known to surfers, as the area in the ocean where you sit in the water while awaiting your next wave to ride.*

Look-at-me Motor bike- *a really loud motorbike or car that seems to scream "LOOK-AT-ME"!!! when you turn the throttle or push the accelerator pedal. A way too loud motorbike or car, with not a whole lot of care for anyone else's ears. But Yucckie has a concept & a solution for this affliction.*

Love- *Love is everything good, love is comfort, caring and honesty, that never leaves anyone lonely sad or hungry. Love is so much more than words can explain. Love is a necessity for all life to succeed. Love is infinite.*

Low pressure system-*An area of a relative pressure minimum that has converging winds and rotates in the same direction as the earth.*

Luck, lucky or luckiness- *Being of fortunate circumstance, is a constant state of mind, Just being able to simply be, one is always quite lucky. To be able to find or create happiness for oneself or another, one is even luckier than most!*

Magnitude- *Great importance: "events of tragic magnitude"*

Mahatma Gandhi- *Mohandas Karamchand Gandhi, 2 October 1869 – 30 January 1948), commonly known as Mahatma Gandhi, was the preeminent leader of Indian nationalism in British-ruled India. Employing non-violent civil disobedience, Gandhi led India to independence and inspired movements for non-violence, civil* rights and freedom across the world. "Be the change" is one of Mahatma Gandhi's more famous quotes.

Martin Luther King Jr.- *Martin Luther King, Jr. (January 15, 1929 – April 4, 1968) was an American clergyman, activist, and prominent leader in the African- American Civil Rights Movement. He is best known for his role in the advancement of civil rights using nonviolent civil disobedience. King has become a national icon in the history of American progressivism.*

Math-a-magical – *Both Yucckie & Mahzie as lover's of the wisdom found in mathematics, feel as if magic is created when one really becomes comfortable with the power of mathematics, which is why they sometimes call mathematical based things "math-a-magical".*

Mctwist- *The McTwist was invented in the early 1980s by skateboarder Mike McGill, and has since been adopted by snowboarders. To perform the trick, the rider does a front flip while at the same time spinning a backside 540. A variety of grabs (most often a mute grab) are used to give the trick more style.*

Meerkats- *The meerkat or suricate, Suricata suricatta, is a small mammal belonging to the mongoose family. Meerkats live in all parts of the Kalahari Desert in Botswana, in much of the Namib Desert in Namibia and southwestern Angola, and in South Africa.*

Mile- *an imperial measurement for long distances – 5,280 feet equal one mile.*

Minjungbal cultural center- *Find it in Tweed Heads Australia*

Morten Bay Fig tree- *Ficus macrophylla, known as the Moreton Bay Fig, is a large evergreen banyan tree of the Moraceae family that is a native of most of the eastern coast of Australia, from the Atherton Tableland (17° S) in the north to the Illawarra (34° S) in New South Wales, and Lord Howe Island. Its common name is derived from Moreton Bay in Queensland, Australia. Individuals may reach 60 m (200 ft) in height. Yucckie believes that Figments of the imagination are born in all Fig trees.*

Morse Code- *An alphabet or code in which letters are represented by combinations of long and short signals of light or sound. Created by Samuel Morse.*

Music- *is an art form whose medium is sound and silence. Its common elements are pitch (which governs melody and harmony), rhythm (and its associated concepts, tempo, meter, and articulation), dynamics, and the sonic qualities of timbre and texture. The word derives from Greek μουσική (mousike; "art of the Muses"). the language of the world, the sound of mathematics. Suggested musicians; Walela, TobyMac, Woody Guthrie, Elizabeth Mitchell, Ziggy Marley, Jack Johnson, Paula Fuga, Stevie Wonder, Renny Field, Zardi, Hera, lead belly, Pharrell Williams, Plum, Aretha Franklin, Bruddah Iz, Cat Stevens, Elton John, Pink, Bob Marley, Michael Franti, Astrud Gilbrerto, The Ventures, The Chantays, Ray Charles, Mark Keali'i Ho'omalu& the Kamehameha school children's chorus, etc.*

Moxy- *incredible great and really happy energy from yourself or* *another person. "You really have Moxy!" Say it to yourself everyday "I really have Moxy!"*

New Butts insulation – *Yucckie and Mahzie believed that because cigarette butts can handle so much direct exposure to heat and other quite scary elements, they collected and cleaned all of the discarded cigarette butts that they could find and used them for insulation in their laptop-shell-cladded-tree-house homes. This work so well that all of the cigarette factories of the world decided to stop making cigarettes and started just making great insulation which caused their butt business to boom!*

No-tox drink – *the best drink for your body on earth, and gift of love known by most as water.*

Not-so-friendly friends- *people that aren't happy with themselves yet, but may probably be your friend one day, when they become happy with themselves.*

Non-flying blue bird- *this is a sad site. When one who has the ability to fly or achieve but choses not to, merely out of fear of the unknown or just simple laziness.*

Om technology – *infinitely open, open-mindedness. Keep an open mind.*

Optimistic – *having the ability to find the good or an opportunity to "do good" with everything.* **Opti-Mystics** – an almost magical way of turning all situations into a joyful learning experience, no matter how difficult it may be.

Out-the-back – *The place known to surfers as the place in the ocean that is much further out then where most of the waves are breaking. Sometimes this is where the really big waves will break due to the depth of the water. (outside or out-the-back)*

Passionate-*is a term applied to a very strong feeling about a person or thing. Passion is an intense emotion compelling feeling, enthusiasm, or desire for something.*

Patience- *is one of the most important ways to be in life, being able to wait for things to happen is an extremely important skill to be great at. It takes many years for a small seed to grow into a massive tree, & so is anything that a person can do that is worthwhile.*

Perplexion- *To be confused or to have trouble with. Uncertainty or doubt.*

Personal space- *Both Yucckie & Mahzie feel that no matter where you are or where you go it is nice to be able to have personal space of at minimum one hula-hoop in circumference around oneself, and if you have even more than that you are doing quite well. If you don't have that much you are quite well off as well, just standing or sitting really close to someone.*

Pessimistic-*A tendency to stress the negative or unfavorable or to take the gloomiest possible view*

Pfffffffffffffftt! – *a sound that some waves make when they spit you out of a wave, Sound that your snowboard makes when perfectly sliding a rail. Also a sound your skate wheels make when sessioning perfectly polished garage concrete.*

PH- words are *special words that are better than words that begin with an "F". Words such as PHat – meaning really amazing or really groovy, PHamous – meaning really amazing people or a really good time, PHriends, meaning the best of the best of friends.*

PHart – *we all do it, and when we do it, it is something to laugh about, as it is a natural bodily function.*

PHrophing – *really, really, really excited (like, turning your guitar or bass amplifier to 12 on a dial that only has 10 settings)*

Phrenzie – *too many people in one place, like in the surf, or on the mountain or even in the food line at the super market trying to get food, ie. feeding phrenzie.*

Pinterest-*A content sharing service that allows members to "pin" images, videos and other objects to their online pin-board.*

Pioneer- *to be on the front of a great change*

Pocket-sized juicer (PSJ) – *it is what it sounds like. Utilized for those emergency juicing situations (EJS).*

Pocohantas- *was the daughter of Powhatan, the paramount chief of a network of tributary tribal nations in the Tidewater region of Virginia. In a well-known historical anecdote, she is said to have saved the life of an Indian captive, Englishman John Smith, in 1607.*

Posting a letter- *the very special caring & loving act of hand* writing between 1 and 4 full pages of paper some of your current feelings for another person or stories about your latest adventures, and then taking the time to fold it, put in in an envelope, sealing it and then buying a special stamp at the post office and sending via the mail to someone that may be just across the street or even on the other side of the world.

Ppapaaahumfp!- *sound that a pounding back-washy shore break can make tell you of a really high-tide.*

Preposterous- *Contrary to reason or common sense; utterly absurd or ridiculous.*

Phonograph- *An early sound-reproducing machine that used cylinders to record as well as reproduce sound.*

Propitious- *Giving or indicating a good chance of success; favorable*

Professor – *"One who professes" and in this case, the fictional name of "P'fessor Guus" is also the current expert on the fictional life, times & adventures of Yucckie & Mahzie. P'fessor Guus was anointed with this nickname by his father when he was just a wee little lad, and this is always remembered and always made him glad.*

Profundity – *a certain depth of profoundness, or insightful wisdom.*

Punctilious- *Showing great attention to detail or correct behavior. Conscientious, diligent, careful & attentive.*

Radio- *An old and current invention that turns transmitted and electromagnetic waves of radio frequency, and those carrying sound messages into audible sound in the form of song, or news messages.*

Recyclable- *reclaimable: capable of being used again or turned into something even better than before.*

Remarkable- *Worthy of attention; striking.*

Sequoia- *(1767–1843), inventor of the Cherokee syllabary, whom all of the following are named after (either directly, or through being named for something named for Sequoyah) – also a place where you can find some of the largest, most blessed, most beautiful trees on earth.*

Scatter gang-*the pack of sheep that always follow and agree with Arrow and Gance especially when they are together on any idea or plan.*

Share Aware (Sharology, Share-ologist) *– One that truly is aware that all the world must best shared, carefully, joyfully and happily, as we are lucky & fortunate to live here on this big blue and green magical planet. Knowing that we are blessed.*

Skateboard- *A short narrow board having a set of four wheels mounted under it, ridden in a standing or crouching position and often used to perform stunts. For some, the act of skateboarding is life.*

Re-smellifier – *specialized recycled baskets that hold fruit skins for utilized for ultra-natural and eco friendly air freshening.*

Skype- *Skype is a software application that allows users to make voice & video calls over the Internet.*

Smoke Signaling-*is one of the oldest forms of long distance communication, it was way of using small puffs of smoke into the sky to message someone far off in the distance.*

Snowboard- *A board resembling a small surfboard and equipped with bindings, used for descending snow-covered slopes on one's feet but without ski poles. For some, the act of snowboarding is life.*
Sojourner Truth- *Sojourner Truth (born 1797 – November 26, 1883) was the self-given name, from 1843 onward, of Isabella Baumfree, an African-American abolitionist and women's rights activist.*

Solar-energy-magnificators – *solar energy re-directing sharing technology. Utilized to share the solar panel power.*

Sound & smell - Triloquism helmets *(hats, hand bags etc.)* – *Specialized sound re- directing devices utilized for re-directing sounds & smells that may cause aggravation to those that do not wish to hear or smell them.*

Spontaneity-*(of a person) Having a natural, and uninhibited manner. the quality of being spontaneous and coming from natural feelings without constraint; "the spontaneity of his laughter".*

Squircle - *a squircle being a bumpy circle endowed with the perfection of imperfections*

Thingamabobicle – a thing, that for an optimistically mind person has many different possibilities of being something useful and new.

S.U.P- *A Stand up paddle-board used for work or recreation in the surf and on flat water.*

Super Foods- *examples of super foods include broccoli, spinach, pumpkin and tomatoes, which are rich in various nutrients. All these fruits and vegetables contain a variety of nutrients and phytochemicals in varying amounts, as do common plant foods like bananas, pineapples and potatoes, which have only rarely been called super foods. Fish may be considered a super food due to their omega-3 fatty acids, which may promote cognitive development.*

Surfing- *The sport or pastime of being carried to the shore on the crest of large waves while standing or lying on a surfboard. For some, surfing is life. Hawaiians believe it to be the sport of Kings.*

Synchronized-*is the coordination of events to operate a system in unison. The familiar conductor of an orchestra serves to keep the orchestra in time.*

T.T. – *tube time a rating for a great experience related to getting a great tube ride while surfing. T.T. is an 11 on a scale of 1 to 10.*

T.T.G.R – *"Tube time in the green room" is actually riding/navigation inside tube of a great wave for a reasonable amount of time – a question might be "Hey how much TTGR have you logged tis year?" More passionate surfers may have logged 2 hours in their whole lifetime, considering the longest of tube rides may be between 6 & 10* seconds of real time.

Tube Riding – *Standing on ones surfboard on the face of a wave, while gravity forces the top of the wave to fall over and fully encircle or ensquircle the surfer of the wave. Tube riding is one of the most sought after and loved experiences for all wave surfers. Some surfers say, Getting tubed is like being born again or even being in the midst of a great time tunnel, where time stands still. Tube riding is also found in snowboarding as the snowboard half pipe is sometime referred to as "the tube".*

Twitter-*is an online social networking service and micro-blogging service that enables its users to send and read text-based messages of up to 140 characters*

Ukulele- *The happiest sounding small four-stringed guitar of Hawaiian origin. This is the gift that keeps on giving. To hear this amazing instrument, Google search – "Bruddah Iz, Some where over the rainbow"*

Ultra-natro-recyclo-friendly- *any substance that is natural and is 100% recyclable*

Unconditional Love- *Unconditional love is a term that means to love someone regardless of the loved one's qualities or actions.*

Unison- *all happening together perfectly*

Universal- *A universal principle is something that exists everywhere; something characteristic of all languages.*

Vernacular- *The language or dialect spoken by the ordinary people in a particular country or region.*

Viber-*lets everyone in the world connect. Freely. Millions of Viber users call, text, and send photos to each other, worldwide- for free.*

Vinegarated clean cleaners – *proprietary eco friendly cleaning solutions using vinegar as a base.*

Vintage- *Too old to be considered modern, but not old enough to be considered antique*

Vision board – *a pin board with which a person can post their greatest future aspirations in an effort to remind themselves of where they would like to be in the future or what they may want to accomplish.*

Wake-skating- *riding a wake skateboard while being towed or towed in by a boat.*

Wikipedia- *an online shared, public, free dictionary. Wikipedia is a free encyclopedia, written collaboratively by the people who use it. It is a special type of website designed to make collaboration easy, called a wiki. Many people are constantly improving Wikipedia, making thousands of changes per hour. All of these changes are recorded in article histories and recent changes*

Wiki-splanation- *explanation by Wikipedia*

W.O.W.O- *Water on, water off – Yucckie's style of showering with a high emphasis on water conservation. Yucckie turns the water on to soak his body, turns it off and soaps up and scrubs down, then brushes his teeth and turns the water on to quickly rinse off, saving nearly a liter or two with every shower leaving more for others that may be in need of one of the most vital resources on earth. I used to think it was because Yucckie would yell out Wow! Ow! when he turned the hot water on by accident, but now even I know why...that is why I love definitions so much.*

You-tube-*is a video-sharing website, created by three former PayPal employees in February 2005, on which users can upload, view and share videos.*

You Ku - *is a video-sharing website in china*

Yucckie & Mahzie – *Best friends to each other & to you & me.*

Zarfo – a unique, Australian designed and created, digital video sharing platform for you i-phone

Z – also *the last letter in the western alphabet*

Bibliography / Disclaimer – some definitions are references from Wikipedia – some definitions are Y&M definitions

If you found any words that your not sure about email Yucckie & Mahzie and they will explain them to you;

Yucckie@yucckie.com or **Mahzie@yucckie.com**

Always remember that "good love" is what we all need. So, if you only want to hear about good things then email Yucckie & Mahzie & for you, I and me, "Good Love" is what they will always return to thee.

Thank you for your time !!!! ☺ ~

Inspirational reading

*A poem @ Minjunbal cultural center -Starfish / author unknown

*The Greatest Salesman in the world

*Reflections of the Christ mind

*The spirit of Tao

General

*Children of the world

*Unconditional Love

Special thanks to; My Wife, Children, father & family, "the Great spirit of love", My friends around the world & all of the great journeys past, present & future to come.

Thank you to; DR. Lee Gibson, Martin Luther King, Mahatma Gandhi, Dartmouth, Mr. Geisel, Dave Cavanagh, Jayson Onley, Rj Williams, Sean & April Slater, Stephen Slater, Kelly Slater, Mark Occhilupo, Layne Beachley, Jenny & Joe D'Orazio, Gretchen Bleiler, Ginny Marie Leines & Leines', The Pospisils, Reto Lamm, Michi Albin, Anne Molin Konsgaard, The Vidals, Sammy Leubke, Chauncey Tanton, Wayne "Rabbit" Bartholomew, Robbie Page, Dave & Shannon Downing, Salema Masekela, David Ni, Juli Shulz, April Hawkins, Sunshine & Judah Mehler, Shanti Sosienski, Susan Izzo, Todd & Lindsey Richards, Jp Walker, JJ Thomas, Piney Kahn, The Nugents, The Fosters, The McCarthys, The MacDonalds, The Buckners, Leslie Wilson Heuer, Mick & Susan Waters, Aiden Foster, Bradley Gerlach, Mike & Allison Arzt, Frank Phillips, John Gerndt, the Geisel family, the Schillings, Kari White, Shaun White, Jessie White, Cathy & Roger White, The Mossop's, The Ciszek Family, Spencer Tamblyn, Shea Perkins, Pheobe Mills, The Hardy's, The Haakonsen's, The Pardoe's, The Wheeler family, Debbie de fiddes, Mike Mcentyre, Karen Low, Wayne Gannon, Andrew

Cunningham, Tj Baron, Dave Keam, Todd Richards, Sarah Graham, Daniel Marlin, Larry Maddox, Todd & Jeannie Chesser, Maya Angelou, Rosa Parks, Piney Kahn, the Bostiks, Peter & Tosh Townend, Jon Flick, Steve Adler, Peter Levin, John Keppler, Mercyships.org, the Sea Shepard, Dustin Barca, Diane Bogui, Kristine Pillai, Kim Harrison, Kate Wagstaff, Deasy Sartika, Andrew Lee, Nicola Conway, Pete & Dustin Del Giudice, the Baker's, Doc Zapalac, Tim Bonython, Scott Needham, Derek Hynd, Jed Done, Jason Bingham, Shagga Siffigna, Philbert, Katie "the dream queen", Jon Foster, Henry Lloyd McCurtis, The Kirby's, Loveland, Craig Kelly, Todd Roberts, Jeff Anderson, Phil Arnott, The Robinsons, Josh Malay, The Warbles, Rainos Hayes, Stacy Schaedler, Sandi Haff, Mark Reeder, Bob Hurley, Al Merrick, Rusty Preisendorfer, Jaime Martin, Heather Dorniden, Davey Miller, Eric Liddell, Harold Abrahams, Joe Mata, Oskari Mykkanen, Sam Luebke, Henning Andersen, Coco Tache, Steve & Tristy Fontes, Natalie Roberts, Michael Weddington, Joker, Bud Keene, Jeff Potto, Virginia Georgeson, Barton Lynch, Eric & Bob Johnson, Steve & Greg Fawley, Dan D'sa, Joel Nelson, Chip Bynum, John Ennis, Sue Izzo, Anna Soss, Greg Strokes, Patrick Mcilvain, Scott Bowers, Mark Scurto, Janet Schnitzler, Al Janc, Jeff Davis, Larry Beard, Billy Morris, Rick Jacovich, Glen Plake, Jonny Herrick, Brent & Kei Futagaki, Rick Lohr, Fran Zi, Mark Albert Holt, Terry Senate, Charlie Wickwire, Duane Toole, Cordell Miller, Ryan & Pat Rawson, Cindy Paragallo, Jay Larson, Lyndon Cabellon, Lisa Hudson, Bruno Musso, Genoveva Hofer, Mark Sperling, John Stouffer, Ian Voterri, Mark Rhodes, Davey Miller, Tina Dixon, Claire Bevilacqua, The Sea Shepard, Green Peace, Planet Ark, Mark Zuckerberg, Matuse, Patagonia, Bruce Lee, John H. Buckner MD, Walt Disney, Muhammad Ali, Jason Cripe, Colin Baden, Brian Takumi, Children's, The Tunnicliffe's, Anna Garcia, Marg Connors, Deb Sphor, Hospitals, Mick, Carol & Dane Hamilton, Todd Mason, Sylvain Garms, Bird Huffman, Miss Hulme, Maria Regina kindy, Bluey's Tree house, The Pearse family, The Grahams, The family Arzt's & Battery 621, Reef & RVCA .

Special Thanks to all contributing artists & editors – RJ Williams, Stan Squire, Nick Lester, Faith, Liberty, Hayley, Gus & John Buckner & also Georgia O'Neill.

Made in the USA
Columbia, SC
27 September 2020

21585583R00105